W9-CJS-293

A BLUE AND GOLDEN YEAR

A BLUE AND GOLDEN YEAR

by

ALISON PRESTON

TURNSTONE PRESS

Copyright © 1997 Alison Preston

Turnstone Press
607–100 Arthur Street
Winnipeg, Manitoba
Canada R3B 1H3

All rights reserved. No part of this book may be reproduced or transmitted in any form or by any means—graphic, electronic or mechanical—without prior written permission of the publisher. Any request to photocopy any part of this book shall be directed in writing to the Canadian Copyright Licensing Agency, Toronto.

Turnstone Press gratefully acknowledges the support of the Canada Council for the Arts and the Manitoba Arts Council for our publishing program.

THE CANADA COUNCIL   LE CONSEIL DES ARTS
FOR THE ARTS   DU CANADA
SINCE 1957   DEPUIS 1957

Cover art: Robert Pasternak

Design: Manuela Dias

This book was printed and bound in Canada by Friesens for Turnstone Press.

Canadian Cataloguing in Publication Data

Preston, Alison, 1949—

A blue and golden year

ISBN 0-88801-206-3

I. Title.

PS8581.R44B48 1997   C813'.54   C97-920025-3
PR9199.3.P725B48 1997

for Dory

Acknowledgements

I would like to thank the following people for their encouragement, advice, practical help, wisdom, and generosity of spirit during the making of this book: David Arnason, John Baillie, Eric Crone, Jacquie Crone, Manuela Dias, Patrick Gunter, Jamie Hutchison, Alexa Milne, David Milne, Marilyn Morton, Robert Pasternak, Graham Shaw, and particularly Caroline Sehon and Wayne Tefs.

Special thanks to John Preston.

Extra special thanks to Bruce Gillespie.

Chapter One
North

Something odd happened shortly after midday, odd in the sense of an unexpected discovery, one that made Arthur's friend Kenneth intensely uncomfortable.

He drove a truck for the city's refuse department. In the mornings he picked up trash from the giant downtown dumpsters and in the afternoons he headed away from the city centre to the industrial park off the south highway and emptied the dumpsters there. Kenneth liked his job. He worked alone and nobody bothered him as a rule. It was always a relief to finish the morning's work, to leave the congestion of downtown streets and get out to the flat quietness of the afternoon.

He was a meticulous worker. If something from a bin missed the truck he got out, picked it up in his huge gloved hands and threw it in. That very thing happened behind a 7-Eleven store as he was getting started on the afternoon portion of his route. He stopped in mid-crouch and recoiled when he saw the movement of legless horrors feeding off something slick. Some of the industrious maggots had entered a ripped seam and their movement out of sight inside the object gave it a life of its own. He wished he had saved his sandwich for later; it wasn't sitting well. When he realized what he was looking at, he knew he had to stop work and phone Arthur.

Chapter Two

Audrey dozed on a lawn chair, her face turned towards the sky. She felt warm and cool, then warm again, as wisps of cloud moved across the sun. She basked tentatively, knowing she oughtn't but unable to resist. Someone said her name and she was suddenly awake, red-faced and grumpy, full of nettlesome dreams.

Lillian stood over her like a thin tower of rags, poking her bony finger into her sister's shoulder. Audrey shuddered as she opened her burnt eyelids.

"What? What do you want?"

She didn't wish that Lillian were dead, but would have been happy never to see her again. She allowed her sister to bring out the worst in her.

"You don't have to shout," Lillian shouted. Then, timidly, "Do you have anything to drink?"

"No." Audrey patted the ground beside her chair, searching for her sunglasses. She found them and put them on. They were held together in the middle with duct tape.

"Nice shades," said Lillian.

"Thanks."

"Come on, Audrey. I'm not feelin' so good." Lillian held her stomach and swayed a little from side to side.

"Well, isn't that unusual. Okay, I've got coffee and I've got one beer and you can't have the beer. I'm saving it."

"Please."

"No. I'm doing you a favour here. You don't look like you'd live through another drink." Audrey squinted up at Lillian for a long moment and then stood up beside her.

"You're actually no longer tall. How can you possibly be shorter than you used to be? Look! I'm taller than you."

"Shut up." Lillian's hands went to her hair, uselessly trying to fluff out the lank grey strands that clung to her head. It was easy to picture the skull beneath the skin, hard not to. The once smooth complexion of her face was a mess of splotches and patches on a dry grey background. She looked dead; the only evidence of life was a trace of something jumpy that came and went in the flat grey eyes; it wasn't much.

They went into the house and Lillian sat slumped in a chair. It was so quiet in the kitchen that Audrey's coffee-making sounds seemed too loud and she found herself setting things down carefully to minimize the racket. She heated a pot of milk on the stove and added some to both their mugs, thinking the straight goods might cause damage.

"I don't want milk."

"Too late." She placed the drink on the table in front of her sister. The mug had I WAS A GUEST ON INFORMATION RADIO emblazoned on the side. Audrey had won it in the Mystery Voice contest.

Lillian gave a shaky sigh and sat back in her chair. The tap dripped and reminded Audrey of all the things that needed doing: the garage door wouldn't close, the cold air vents had all become unattached from the walls, the yard was a mess.

Lillian's eyes were closed and she looked as though she might vanish into the wallpaper, she appeared so insubstantial. The healthy plants and busy paraphernalia of the room seemed to move in and almost obliterate her weakened form. Audrey was shocked that her kitchen could overpower someone in this way; she stared.

"No, that's just silly."

"What?" Lillian's eyes opened.

"Nothing." Audrey tried unsuccessfully to stop the constant drip of the tap. She adjusted the dishcloth under it so she wouldn't have to hear it anymore.

"Iggy kicked me out." Lily's monotone interrupted Audrey's mental list-making. She wanted to spruce up a few areas in her yard and was hatching various simple plans, ones that wouldn't involve too much work.

"Who's Iggy?" She forced herself into the conversation.

"Jesus. Don't you pay any attention to my life?"

"I try not to," she replied honestly. "Who's Iggy?"

"He's the dude I've been living with for the last four months. We were really serious about each other."

"Dude?"

"Yeah."

"Whatever happened to Lenny or Squiggy or whatever his name was who showed up with you on Christmas?"

"Lanny. Never mind. I'm leaving." Lillian dragged herself up and moved towards the door. Her jeans were held up by a piece of rope and the only sign from the back that there was anything inside them was a pair of skinny ankles sticking out the bottom.

"What's the matter? You haven't even touched your coffee. I went to all that trouble. I used the last of my milk." Audrey flattened the carton and pitched it in the general direction of the door where there was a small pile of stuff on its way to other places. It hit Lillian in the foot.

"Ow!"

"Sorry."

"I shouldn't have come here. You hate me. You'd be glad if I was dead." Lillian's hand was on the doorknob, her eyes were on nothing. Her shoulders turned in on herself as if to encircle and protect her heart and other soft spots.

Audrey was disgusted with her own behaviour. "I'm sorry."

Lillian looked at her warily. "You're not sorry. You just feel guilty."

Their eyes met for a second and Audrey felt her face heat up. "Come on back, Lily, finish your coffee and tell your nasty little sister all about it."

"It's funny," said Lillian, "I don't feel guilty about stuff. I feel lots of really horrible other things but not guilt."

"Well, you can't have everything," Audrey grinned.

Lillian didn't grin back but sat down looking so beaten that Audrey marvelled once more at the difference between them, two sisters barely twelve months apart. One was born happy and lucky, the other, desperate and struggling, it seemed like always and forever, from the moment she landed with a thud from the same warm place that ushered Audrey into the world. Audrey knew that Lillian hated her for it. She supposed she loved her, too, somewhere deep down, but not as much as she hated her.

She remembered a time when they were very young, six and seven maybe, when she had discovered Lillian in front of the full-length mirror in their parents' bedroom. She had been practising, saying things like "Hi, guys" and "Is that ever neat!" in a perky unfamiliar voice. Audrey had run from the scene, awash in the greatest fear and sadness she had known up to that point in her short life.

Now Lillian looked at her coffee and said, "I hate milk." She shook like someone in the last stages of Parkinson's disease.

"Okay, okay." Audrey threw it down the sink and poured her a fresh mug. Her uneasiness grew; her sister was a wreck.

"So, why did Iggy kick you out?"

"Oh, what happened wasn't really important. He isn't even that important to me anymore. It's that I literally have nowhere to go." She gave Audrey a quick glance.

Oh no, thought Audrey. "So, what did happen though?"

"Oh, he's got this thing about his possessions, his stuff. He collects things and I guess I don't take it seriously enough to make him happy. I broke one of his model cars. I was babysitting the kid next door—"

"Wait. You were babysitting?"

"Yeah. The kid and I get along. His name is James, he calls himself Steve, but I call him Waldo. He's a seven-year-old beatnik, a good reader. We read out loud together. And stop being so astounded every time you hear something about me that isn't horrible."

Audrey stared; it sounded far too normal. And Lillian was showing signs of animation. Was this real? she wondered. Why would she make up something like that, unless it was just some new exercise in weirdness?

Lillian took a tiny sip of coffee and shuddered.

"How about some toast or cereal or—"

"No! No, coffee's great, thanks." She took another sip. "Anyway, we can't read all the time and Iggy's models are kinda like toys. We broke one and for Ig it was the last straw. He flipped his lid and told me to get out."

"It sounds like he overreacted. Maybe it wasn't really the last straw. Maybe he was just feeling grumpy. Have I got all the facts?" she asked, not wanting any more. She had a feeling she would be dragged down into the depths of despair.

And she wasn't entirely unsympathetic to Iggy. She thought about her books. To a casual observer they may have looked haphazard and dog-eared, but to Audrey her collection was in perfect order, not to be trifled with.

"Audrey," Lillian interrupted her sister's righteous reverie, "I wouldn't ask if I wasn't desperate."

"Oh no, Lily." She squeezed her eyes shut.

"Can I stay here for one or two nights till I get things figured out?"

"No, please."

"Please. You won't even know I'm here. I won't wreck anything, I promise."

Audrey opened her eyes; her face hurt from the sun. "How could I not know you're here? You stink, for Christ's sake. Lily, please don't ask this of me. I'm not a nice enough person to put you up for a day or two. Look what happened to us the last time we tried living together. I mean, I'm having trouble with just this short visit."

In fact, the two sisters had lived together over a bitterly cold winter back in the early seventies. It hadn't gone well.

They split apart just before the spring thaw. Audrey made the move because she was afraid they would kill each other.

"This wouldn't be like that. It would only be for a day or two."

Tears sprung to Lillian's eyes but Audrey didn't notice. "You try to make it all sound so normal, your life, what you do, but you're fucked up. You're leaving out the real parts, and the thing is, I don't want to know them. You look like you should be hospitalized, for Christ's sake. Any emergency room with one look at you would take you in for at least a couple of days, in spite of cutbacks. Or go back to Iggy and grovel," she added brightly. "That might work."

Audrey was greedy with her solitude; sharing wasn't something that came easily to her. She thought about her years with Terence. Her sharing abilities weren't very finely honed during that period; they had existed so separately from one another. And when they had managed to come together there were too many sharp edges between the two of them to provide for any real comfort.

The phone rang. Audrey took advantage of it, she needed a break. The caller easily talked her into a free pair of windshield wipers. She made a great display of welcoming the stranger to her home, giving him detailed directions. She wasn't paying attention to him but rather to the guilt that rooted in her stomach and swelled up inside her. It exhausted her. She hung up the phone, put her head down on the table, and went to sleep.

When she woke up twenty minutes later Lillian was still there.

"You can stay for one night. And you have to behave yourself. Tomorrow I'm having someone over for dinner and you have to be gone before I start getting ready. The couch in the sunroom pulls out."

The part about a dinner guest was a lie but she could always rustle someone up if it came to that, the windshield wiper salesman if need be. She was getting seriously depressed. It was time to get moving.

"So, how are you going to spend the rest of the day?" Audrey ventured.

"I don't know. Does it matter?"

"Well no, I guess not. I'm just trying to get the lay of the land. Are you going out? Will you need a key? Should I show you how the alarm system works? Will you be inviting any criminals over while I'm out?"

"No."

"No?"

"Yeah, no."

Audrey sighed and headed off to the shower. Her eyelids stung. She hoped she hadn't done any permanent damage to the complicated infrastructure that held her face together. She ran the hot water until she was warmed through, then turned it to cold and shivered in wretched discomfort. This was her habit, enacted twice, once at the beginning and then at the end of her shower, running the hot just long enough to get comfortable and then dashing cold water down upon herself. Her showers were satisfying but she would have been hard pressed to expain her ritual to anyone else.

The face in the mirror was plain but pleasing when she smiled. Her features weren't well defined like Lillian's. She thought she looked as though her mouth and nose had been thrown at her face in passing, making them slightly off kilter and a bit smashed-in looking.

Maybe it'll be okay, she said to the mirror. Maybe this horrid feeling in the pit of my stomach doesn't really belong there.

She laid down a few ground rules before heading out. No smoking, no scaring the cat, no long-distance phone calls. Lillian shrugged and Audrey felt sick as she walked out to her car. Her neighbour, Arthur Pointe, was lying in his hammock strung between two poplars in his yard. She smiled to herself at the sight.

Arthur was feeling something close to rapture as he watched the light play through the new leaves. Nothing took the sun quite like a poplar tree. He'd had a trying couple of days since Kenneth had come by. Disquieting thoughts had been swirling round and round his brain, when the beauty of the trees stepped in to calm him.

"Hi, Arthur," Audrey shouted, and gave a little salute when he raised his head.

"Hello, Audrey. How are you?" He had heard raised voices earlier from over the fence and hoped everything was okay. He knew how Audrey cherished her weekends.

She sighed. "Okay, thanks. I'll see ya later."

He was close enough to notice that she was out of sorts. Only the bottom half of her face was smiling. Ah well. Perhaps she would want to talk later. He waved his so-long and lay back down.

But clouds had moved to block the sun and the trees had become quite ordinary in the new light. When Arthur found his mind going back to his recent difficulties he knew it was time to get up. He dumped himself out onto the ground and made his way slowly to the small shed where he kept his gardening tools. Perhaps he could work the thoughts of Nate Underhill out of his system.

Audrey drove to the nursery. Her car wasn't making any extra sounds; it had been behaving itself for a few months and that made her happy.

Terence entered her thoughts again, and the days leading up to her decision, the way she had felt on that night ten years earlier when she had realized it was time to go. She had sat by the window and waited. She liked waiting; it was like a gift of time. People who knew Audrey and cared about her thought Terence was inconsiderate. They didn't think she should spend so much time waiting for him, but she honestly didn't care.

She rolled down both windows in her car to allow for the fresh spring air.

She had waited that evening for him to come home so they could go out again. It wasn't dark yet, it was June, and the view from her window reminded her of "The Hissing of Summer Lawns" by Joni Mitchell so she played it. She knew then that she would be leaving soon. It was a happy thought and she was amazed it had never occurred to her before. She felt light and airy and changed her clothes to suit her mood. Terence wouldn't like the gauzy display but she didn't have to care anymore.

Audrey pictured how she had looked on that long-ago summer night and smiled. She'd worn pink sandals.

She had walked home alone, insisted on it. It would have been more pleasant if Terence hadn't followed along in the car, shouting at her to get in goddamnit. She had laughed though and been pleased with herself for working and saving her whole life. She could look for a small house, put down a payment; a house with a porch.

Now, pulling a wagon behind her, Audrey picked out petunias, lobelia, a tray of day lilies, and a lilac shrub that one day would smell heavenly on warm spring mornings. Mornings like the one she had been enjoying today before her sister ruined it. She could plant it right up against the porch.

"That oughta do me," she said out loud, as she laid everything gently in the back of her station wagon.

She decided to drop the plants off but stopped first for a jug of milk and a fudgsicle. The idea of Lillian in her house alone made her nervous. She felt unsafe with her around, as though her house might suddenly catch fire through faulty wiring or its foundation crumble because of the odd cast of the earth beneath it. She knew that Lillian's intentions held little or no malice, but still, there was something there that frightened Audrey and worried her, something old.

A bothersome memory came to her. It was her birthday, her ninth or tenth, and she came upon Lillian in the basement working hard at creating something. She had made little plaster moulds of the Duck family: Donald, Daisy,

Huey, Dewey, Louie, and Uncle Scrooge McDuck. She was painting them carefully with a comic book beside her as a guide. Audrey made fun of her, especially of her choice of subjects. She figured if a person was going to make stupid little plaster figures, they should at least be of fabulous characters like Katy Keene or Milly the Model. She never saw the finished product and realized when the day was over and she hadn't received a gift from Lillian that the ducks had been for her. And the worst part, as she remembered that little episode from her past, was that she hadn't felt badly at the time about her own insensitivity, but rather about the lack of a present from Lillian.

Audrey shuddered. She hated remembering things that cast her in a bad light. It happened all the time. She wanted to go home to Lillian now and throw her arms around her and apologize about the ducks. But she wouldn't, of course.

She threw her fudgsicle out the window after a few bites. It didn't taste as good as she wanted it to.

Where the hell had her parents been during the duck fiasco? Why hadn't they taken her aside and shaken her and explained about people's feelings? Her mother would have been gone already and her dad would have been drunk or at the office. She should have known anyway. Children aren't born mean are they? It seemed to Audrey a bizarre world where people had to be carefully taught not to be cruel.

When she saw the police car turn onto her street she knew it would stop at her house. It was an unmarked car but had a detachable flashing light sitting atop the passenger side. She was filled with dread and humiliation, as in "How could she do this to me?" It amazed her that all her pettinesses stayed put when something serious happened.

She decided too late to keep on driving. The cop on the driver's side had seen her and he gave a friendly wave. There were good things about living in a small city, but Audrey wasn't sure if having gone to school with members of the police force was one of them. Frank Foote had been her boyfriend in grade eleven and her first real lover. There were some enchantments and clumsy fumblings with others but Frank was the one, hard-pressed as he was to believe it at the time. She hadn't seemed to be a virgin, which puzzled them both. It made things easy, physically, but Frank seemed hurt and Audrey didn't yet know how to apologize for things that weren't her fault. He got over it without too much trouble, being an easygoing guy and wanting badly to believe her. That was well over a quarter of a century ago but Audrey still used his gentle and curious ways in her imaginings.

She didn't see him often, the city wasn't that small, but his older daughter was her paper girl, and Audrey enjoyed that small connection. Em came around every day after school, pushing her cart, always polite and willing to talk if Audrey made any effort at all. It amazed Audrey that a girl her age would read the newspaper she delivered, voraciously even, and want to talk about the insanity reported on its inky pages. She seemed so young to care so much about things that weren't directly related to her own life.

Em didn't see it that way, she was smart enough to realize that it was all connected, that it affected her in deep and mysterious ways. Unemployment statistics, dwindling health care funds, the quality of city air, she worried about it all, sensing the uncertainty of her future and the well-being of those close to her. The interconnectedness of the news fascinated her. She knew that the increase in violent crime was a direct result of the other more political-sounding stories. She said that if she was in charge at the newspaper she would lay things out more imaginatively, to demonstrate those links. She would get to the heart of the matter.

Audrey tipped her rather grandly at Christmas time, she didn't know what else to do for her.

She licked the corners of her lips, hoping that she didn't have fudgsicle on her face, as she opened the back of the wagon to give her plants more breathing room. She felt a stirring inside herself as Frank strode toward her. He was a tall man, six feet two inches, and the weight he had gained since the days of his youth only improved his appearance, made him more huggable and substantial looking. A dependable man. She hoped the flush she felt on her face wasn't visible on the outside. Then she remembered her sunburn and gave up any thoughts of trying to look cool and pretty.

"Audrey. I'm glad you drove up. Are you okay?" He touched her shoulder. She was glad he wasn't paying attention to the hands-off manifesto of the nineties. The smile on his handsome face reminded her of when she had introduced him to Lily years before and her response had been a suspicious "He *seems* nice enough. . . ."

"Well, except for my baked face." She put her hands up to her cheeks. "Why? What on earth's going on, Frank? What's with the light?" She looked around her nervously. "I like to try to seem normal to my neighbours."

Frank shouted, "Turn off the light, Freddy, and shut the car off." He turned to Audrey. "I'm really sorry, I didn't even realize."

The street was quiet. Not even Dicky Putz' lawnmower roared through the still clean air. It was possible that the wielders of summer machinery were taking breaks while there was something to be observed from behind their caraganas and aluminum mini-blinds.

"Actually, we're looking for Lillian," said Frank. "Have you seen her lately?"

"Let's sit down. I'll get us some coffee." Audrey started transporting her plants to the porch and Frank took the milk and went over to speak to Fred. She hoped he wasn't inviting him in. In amongst all the difficulty she had a happy desire to make café au lait for her old boyfriend and didn't want to include a crumby little cop named Fred.

She waited in the porch, messing around with her plants. Fred drove off and Frank came in and sat awkwardly on her red wooden stool.

"Could you wait here a sec, Frank?"

"Sure." He crossed his arms and had a look around. He had never been there before.

She took the milk and went inside. The door was open. She looked around for Lillian. It took seconds for her to realize she wasn't there. Good. Her anger at the unlocked door vanished amidst new hope that Lillian wouldn't be back.

Audrey was setting up the coffee when Frank knocked on the door.

She had a quick look around to make sure nothing of her sister remained. "Come on in."

Frank smiled at her affectionately and sat in one of the straight pine chairs on top of a bag of clothespegs. She put out some homemade coconut cookies that looked like odd little sea creatures. Oh, how she wished it were just a social visit!

Frank said, "I sure do wish this was just a social visit." She presented him with his coffee and sat down across the table.

"Okay, what's up Frank?"

He busied himself with arranging the clothespegs more comfortably beneath him. Audrey took them off his hands and sat back down, beaming at him.

Frank remembered quite clearly the complicated dynamics at work in Audrey's family home when he had first come to know her. The mother was long gone by then. (She had left a note, pleading with her small family to be able to get along without her.)

He had rarely glimpsed Mr. Laird, but could picture him still, peeking out from behind his three-piece suit and bottle of gin.

"Howdy, Frankie, how's tricks?" he would slur and Frankie responded, always polite, always calling him sir.

They'd had the odd true exchange while he was vulnerable, in the throes of fierce hangovers. "Girls shouldn't have to grow up without their mothers, Frankie, but Audrey's okay, don't you think?"

"Yes sir, she sure is."

"I worry about Lily though. She's got a streak in her."

But mostly he was full of stinky bluster, boasting of friends in high places, of hobnobbing with generals and such. He was a WW2 man and to him military heroes were the top of the barrel. They were the worthy ones. He droned on and on about the war like no other dad that Frank knew. "You kids can't understand what it was like for us. I killed people, Frankie," he would say, staring at his hands, as though he had used them to strangle countless soldiers. For all Frank knew, he had.

It wasn't hard for Frank to see how a woman could have wanted to run from him and never come back; harder perhaps to understand how she could have left her two small daughters in his care. It's difficult to know what goes on inside someone else. Love, hate, indifference are all camouflaged by the dailiness of life. The way Audrey had described Mrs. Laird made her sound like anyone else's mother. She bundled them up for school, made lunch and tucked them into bed at night. She didn't bother with the PTA or coffee mornings, but many mothers didn't.

Audrey and Lillian had managed. Their grandmother had been there for a while after their mother left, their father's mother, but that had been more like having another child around the house. She shopped for them and that was about it. The groceries she brought home were unusual, things they had never seen before, like caviar and head-cheese, and potatoes and carrots in jars. The everyday vegetables took on a sinister quality in liquid in glass and the sisters chased each other with them, pretending they were pickled body parts. They would spring them on each other suddenly, shrieking with terrified hilarity as they tore through the house, slamming out the front door and across the neighbours' lawns.

Grandmother Laird moved to the coast in the early sixties. Audrey and Lillian took it personally and they might not have been far wrong. But after she had gone they found they didn't miss her, the only things she had provided were the groceries.

After that Oliver Laird bought care for his daughters in the form of one housekeeper after another till the girls were in their mid-teens. Audrey was embarrassed by her father and she seldom allowed a friend near the house, except for Frank; he had seemed to get the picture clearly and had played no small part in easing her pain.

"Do you see much of Lillian these days?" Frank asked now.

"No." Audrey was pushing the cookies around on the plate as though there was a special formation required that she hadn't quite mastered.

"Do you know where she is, how she's doing?"

"Frank, for Christ's sake, let's have it!" Cookies leapt off the plate at her abruptness. "Did she steal something, was she drunk and disorderly, has she been caught soliciting, did she shoot someone . . ."

"Okay, okay!" Frank placed the flyaway treats back on the plate. "A man called Ignatius Strand has been killed. Lillian knew him, probably lived with him."

Audrey stared at Frank. He went to the sink and got her a glass of water.

"What do you mean killed?"

"Killed, as in murdered, I'm afraid."

She sipped the water. "What do you mean murdered?"

"Murdered, as in offed, snuffed, you know, murdered. And it looks like Lillian may have been living with him, from stuff we've found in his apartment."

"Oh dear. Well, I don't . . . didn't know anyone called Ignatius Strand. I don't even really know Lillian very well anymore. There's probably not a heck of a lot I can tell you."

Murder. I'm involved in a murder, Audrey thought. I'll have to testify, like I've known all my life I'd have to do. And I'll fuck it up and go to jail. There'll be a lie, an accidental lie like the one I told just now, and then I'll go to jail where I'll be forced to have sex with big matrons with forks.

"Cookie?" she offered.

She watched as Frank munched away with a look of deep concentration on his face.

"Hey, these are good!" he said as he reached for another one.

"You sound surprised."

"Well, it's just that they look kind of funny."

"Yeah, they don't look quite like they did in the picture." Audrey munched too for a bit and then said, "Where's Fred?"

"I told him to drive around and phone me here after a little while. I hope that's okay."

"Sure." Maybe I can fake my death and go to Rio, thought Audrey.

"Now, where were we?"

"We were talking about Fred. How is he, as partners go?"

Frank laughed. "Come on Audrey. This is serious. We have to talk about your sister."

"Yeah, okay."

"Have you seen her lately?"

She told Frank about her morning visitor, still leaving out the parts about Iggy, and Lillian's intention to stop off for a couple of days. He seemed to believe her when she said she didn't know where her sister had gone; after all, it was true.

The phone rang. It was right there in the kitchen so Audrey was desperate for it not to be Lillian. It was Fred. She turned to Frank, who was staring at her.

"It's you-know-who for you-know-who."

He whispered "Nice outfit" as he took the phone from her hand.

She was glad she had settled on her periwinkle tee shirt. She gave him her best smile and left the room so he could talk privately to his buddy.

Audrey looked out the living-room window with her hands deep in her overalls' pockets. She had known her sister was a bit of a mess but had always figured that ultimately she would be okay. She wondered if that had just been an excuse for ignoring her.

They had been a team at one point in their lives, wild best friends. They started drinking in high school, mainly just weekends and summers, but Lillian always needed it more than Audrey. That was what life was to her, booze and boys. Audrey always had something else going on, like the school paper and the job she took at Dodd's Pharmacy so she could buy records. Those things guided her in putting the limits on herself that a gin-sodden father couldn't.

Lillian didn't have that built-in sensibleness and her behaviour was often extreme or downright odd. Like the August night she ran naked down their quiet residential street. Nobody dared her, she was quite alone. It was late, around three in the morning, so no one saw her except the police who happened to be cruising down the avenue of elms where the Lairds lived. A uniformed cop took her to her door and presented her to Mr. Laird, who was astonished at the time, but didn't remember it in the morning. But the morning after that, it was in the local paper, name and all (Lillian had just turned eighteen), so the family experienced a sort of celebrity status for a while.

Audrey had asked her about it and Lillian said, "I don't know. It was just so hot. I couldn't sleep and the street looked so beautiful from my bedroom window, still and empty except for me. I wanted to be naked in it."

She would do anything and pushed the limits further when the summer of love introduced drugs to the little Canadian city. Audrey was in university and Lillian was working lousy jobs, adrift on a sea of mind alterations. They still hung around together sometimes, but Audrey, while trying it all (even heroin once), managed to keep it recreational, while Lillian used it as a life. She did stints in the psychiatric wing of one of the city hospitals, supposedly trying to get off the stuff, but she was turfed out for good when she was found in a tiny supply room with a beautiful summer orderly. They were high as the sky and, of course, naked.

18

It got so the sisters saw little of each other. When their paths did cross Audrey wondered at the strength of Lillian's constitution, at a body and brain that were able to take such prolonged battering. Lillian put no limits on herself. Sometimes Audrey envied her that, her seeming ability not to give a shit, to be able to wake up every morning and fall back into a life with no boundaries, no responsibilities, no lists, no rules. Audrey almost ruled herself to death sometimes. She made the free space around her so small that she couldn't get a breath.

Frank came into the living room. "Thanks, Audrey. Freddy'll be around to pick me up in a few minutes."

"Great. Maybe this time he'll turn the siren on too."

"I'm really sorry about that. Honest, I didn't even notice that he had the light going." Frank sat on a wobbly little footstool. "Now, maybe we could use these few minutes for you to bring me up to date on Lily."

He always seemed to pick the most uncomfortable place to sit. Audrey's cat, Craig, was like that. If he didn't get to sit on Audrey for some reason, he sat on little pointed edges or cluttered surfaces or even in cool drafts. Weird behaviour in a cat or a man! Audrey thought Craig did it to make her feel guilty but with Frank it couldn't be that. It was probably something far less complex.

He continued, "At this point, she's the only lead we have. We're not suspecting her of having killed him or anything."

"Really?"

"No. Of course not. We just have to find people who knew him so we can get some kind of handle on his life."

"Why didn't you say so? I don't know what the Christ I'm supposed to be thinking."

"Sorry. It hadn't even occurred to me that you would think that."

Audrey sat down on the couch with her feet up and her arms hugging her knees.

Frank continued, "He was killed at home and we don't think it was random violence, although at this point we don't know for sure."

"Please don't keep saying 'we.' It makes me feel like my remarks are going to be right out there for all and sundry to browse through and analyze. Are they?"

"No. Not unless it's a remark that's obviously connected to the case." Frank stood up and moved to the couch, where he sat down beside her. "I'm really sorry about this, Audrey. Try not to worry, okay?"

"How was he killed?"

Frank hesitated. "It was pretty grim. Are you sure you want to know?"

"Oh dear. No. But you'd better tell me anyway." She braced herself by pressing her feet against Frank's leg and sitting on her hands.

"Are you sure?"

"Fra-ank. Let's have it. And quickly please."

"He was killed with a garrote. He was garroted."

"Garroted! Good heavens! It sounds like something Ruth Rendell would dream up."

"Who's Ruth Rendell?"

"Never mind. Go ahead."

"Actually, it's not all that uncommon these days. Death is usually by strangulation but it can be caused by damage to the spinal cord right at the top where it joins the brain."

"Okay. Okay. I get it."

"The weapon is usually a strong cord or a wire with handles at both ends to make the job easier. In this case it was probably a wire, judging from how the wound looked, but we're waiting for all the official death reports."

"Yuck. Could you please not talk about it anymore for the moment?"

"Sorry."

Audrey gave pause to the idea of Frank examining a horrible neck wound on a dead man. He was so matter-of-fact about it, this man who had guided her so tenderly in that most important act of life all those years ago. He had touched dead people since then, examined their wounds with the same careful attention that he had paid her willing young body. At that time he hadn't known he was going to be a cop. He had worked on weekends for an exterminator and assumed that was where his future lay. Audrey remembered being mildly grossed out by how he spent his Saturday mornings.

"So they didn't find the weapon . . . the garrote?" Audrey's hands had come free but her feet remained pressed up against Frank.

"No."

"Why has it become such a popular way to kill someone?"

"Well, for one thing the murderer can sneak up from behind and not have to look at the victim's face. And also, it can be a real ambush, creeping up like that. We're sure, sorry, I'm sure, that Mr. Strand was taken by surprise. He'd been wearing headphones. Plus, he was sitting on a high stool kind of like your red wooden one on the porch. He made a perfect target."

Audrey began to get a little trembly; she sat up so her feet were on the floor. Frank touched her forearm and she leaned into him just a little. She wanted him to touch her face, or at least her hair, but he didn't.

"Are you all right, Aud?" He was the only person in her life who had ever shortened her name to Aud and she liked it. It made her feel like a person with a nickname, a popular person who had been a cheerleader in high school.

"Yeah, I'm okay. How did you guys find him? Did somebody report it?"

"Yeah, we got an anonymous tip. Someone just said, 'Dead guy,' gave the address, and hung up. The call came from the apartment but it was hard to tell if it was a man or woman. It's on tape but that's not much help. The person used a really gruff voice, you know, forming the words right in their throat." Frank gave a demonstration of how he thought it was done.

Audrey laughed, "Very good, Frank."

Audrey and Lillian had talked to each other like that when they were kids and driven strangers crazy. It hurt after only a short while but it was an enormous amount of fun. They did it on the bus behind meek-looking people sitting alone. They were relentless and confident that their victim would be too shy to complain. They did it at movies during quiet moments and drove people to shout "Shut up!" angrily towards the back of the theatre where they sat giggling. How rude they were! They even did it from the balcony of the church where they sat on endless Sunday mornings in a slaphappy effort to get their CGIT points. The minister finally kicked them out and told them never to come back. They pretended to go to church for a while after that, imagining that it mattered to their father, but when they realized it didn't, they stopped.

The doorbell rang.

Frank said, "Shit." They moved back into the kitchen and he went to the door, where Fred kept trying to peer past him into the house. Frank told him to wait in the car and assured him he wouldn't be long. Fred looked a little morose as Audrey watched him walk down the sidewalk.

"Okay, Audrey, is there anything else you think I should know? What's her story? Is she into the hard stuff? I haven't seen her for so long I'm not even sure I'd recognize her."

"What would make you say that about the hard stuff?"

"Well, there was stuff in the apartment that made it look a bit like a user's home. No drugs, mind you, but a bit of paraphernalia."

"I honestly don't know. And as far as recognizing her, you probably wouldn't." Audrey thought of Lily's pointed little face and felt like crying. "Could I get back to you? I think I should ponder this a bit, and I could try to talk to you later today if that's okay? Maybe I can talk to somebody, her maybe."

"Okay, good. Uh, we may have to talk to your dad."

"Oh Christ. Could you please not do that? It'll be useless. Believe me, at best, it'll be totally useless."

Frank looked discomfited.

"Please, not yet, anyway."

"I can't promise, Audrey, but I won't initiate anything. I

better get going. I hope I hear from you. I'm on till six. If you phone the station they'll give any message to me right away. If you want to phone me at home after that, that's okay too."

"Doesn't your family mind your being bothered at home?"

"They're used to it. And in your case it wouldn't be a bother, it'd be a pleasure. Please call."

"So long Frank."

"Adios. Take it easy. Try not to worry, and call me even if you don't have anything for me, just to talk if you want. See ya."

Frank left, and Audrey felt bereft. It wasn't so much that she wanted to sleep with him or marry him or blow up his family. It was the past she thought of, wondering if she had paid more attention then, if her memories would be clearer. Likely. But then, hurts would probably be deeper too. Maybe she had been paying more attention. She ran outside and shouted, "Frank."

He turned around with his hand on the car door handle.

"What was Iggy listening to on the headphones?"

Frank looked disappointed. "I don't know. I'll find out. Phone me, Audrey."

They drove away slowly and Audrey turned to her new plants. She wasn't up to putting them in just yet but she watered each one carefully and placed it near the ground where it would go. She didn't want her family shared with Fred and hoards of other strangers. Frank knew that but also knew he couldn't control it. She felt sorry for him but worse for herself, and her sorriness knew no bounds when it came to Lillian.

She dragged a huge bag of peat moss from the garage and searched the porch for her trowel and kneeling cushion. Getting ready was half of it. If her equipment sat waiting for her, it would be easy to plop down at a moment's notice and start work.

Audrey hoped fervently they would leave her father alone. Oliver Laird hadn't stopped drinking as long as she had known him. His mind was a confused mess with holes in it. He embellished his life with far-flung ideas that gave it enough drama to get him through his lonely days. The Lillian thing would be something terrible to sink his teeth into, to keep him company as he drank his private toasts. But being the father of a girl who knew a dead guy wouldn't be enough. He would hint at sinister connections and previous mistakes in his daughter's life until only a miracle or a perceptive cop could interrupt his blazing trail of witless destruction. Audrey shuddered and shook herself free. She needed a walk and a sit by the river.

Chapter Three
South

Ignatius Strand woke up unrested. In his dream he had killed someone and it took him the better part of a minute to understand that he was awake. His intention had been to turn his world into a place where he could be comfortable again but he felt unsure of himself and his plans, and wondered if he even knew what comfort was. He was pretty sure he had liked himself at one time but he couldn't remember who he had been then.

He noticed that he wasn't alone and the night came back to him. The beautiful girl (she couldn't have been more than seventeen) had been everything he'd wanted, but with the morning he wanted her gone.

He sighed and kissed a smooth brown arm before heading off to a scalding shower, as hot as he could stand it. Even in the late spring heat he didn't feel warm. There was a small blizzard inside him and he didn't know how to make it go away.

The girl crept out before he returned. He had given her fifty American dollars and she was pleased.

He phoned room service for coffee. This hotel was the only one he knew of right in the town that provided that luxury. The swanky places were a few miles down the beach, but he liked being in the noisy heart of things.

His balcony looked down on a scruffy courtyard. There

were people moving about and he recognized Juan, the hotel handyman who had fixed his shower yesterday. He sat on a stump drinking from a cup, watching a tired-looking woman peg laundry to a line. And children, six of them, all looking under ten years old, worked or played or slept under the watchful eye of their mother. Behind them was a lean-to. No matter how hard he tried Iggy couldn't see it as more than that. It was a tiny home of old wood and cloth. Two skinny dogs nosed about and a rooster marched forthrightly. Iggy remembered being awakened by a cocka-doodle-doo but had thought it was part of his dream.

Juan stretched and looked up. Iggy was embarrassed and gave a feeble wave. Juan smiled a big smile and waved back, maybe on account of the generous tip Iggy had given him. He spoke to his wife and she also smiled and waved. Then several children noticed and joined in the waving and giggling too. When the rooster began to crow Iggy stepped back inside.

He decided not to shave, contemplated growing a full beard. In the early days with Lily her chin was always red and raw. She was so crazy about him she didn't complain but she did talk about the benefits of grown-out whiskers. Even if he shaved just before, her sensitive skin told the story the next day. That and her beautiful swollen lips. Oh Christ, Lily, I did care about you. Do. Maybe without him she'd grab onto a lifeline. What else could he allow himself to think?

He got dressed. First, the money belt which he took from under the mattress. Stupid to have left the girl alone with it but he didn't think. He was going to have to get better at that sort of thing. Again his misgivings niggled him when he saw a lifetime of extreme caution stretched out ahead. He hoped to feel better about things after getting the money settled in somewhere. It was the paranoia, the constant fear and uneasiness that he was supposed to be running away from. Perhaps it wouldn't be so easy.

He slipped into a white cotton shirt and pants, loose

summer clothes. When he glanced in the mirror he didn't like what he saw. His thin face was pale; he needed a tan.

Maybe Mexico was a bad idea. Everything felt dangerous to him, like he was one step away from jail or death. It had something to do with the weather. Switzerland would have been a better choice. He had all the right papers with the name Paul Syms in place of his own. It wasn't the first time he had used an alias; he could still go.

He looked for a little restaurant remembered from many winters ago. It was very early and very hot. Just a few of the locals moved about and there wasn't a tourist in sight. Only misfits and drug dealers came to Mexico in late spring. Yes, perhaps a cooler clime.

The restaurant was still there and he had more coffee, fried eggs and Canadian bacon. The bacon was great, far better than any he'd ever had in Canada. The eggs weren't so good. He guessed it was the butter they were fried in. The butter here often made him feel kind of funny. Maybe the cows grazed differently than they did back home. Maybe they were goats.

What to do next. He had two choices: find a good safe place for his money or get out, perhaps to Scotland by way of Switzerland. He was whistling "Speed Bonny Boat" as he left the restaurant and walked straight into the huge bulk of Big Heap Huggins.

"How ya doin', Ig?" Heap shouted with joy and punched him in the shoulder hard enough that Iggy threw up his arms to protect himself from further good-natured abuse.

"Hi, Heap, how's it going?" He rubbed his shoulder and backed off slightly.

"What are you doing here? It's been years, man. Are you alone? On holidays? Let's go down to the beach for a brewsky and you can tell me all about it."

"Thanks Heap. I'd like that but there're some things I've got to do this morning." Iggy checked his watch.

"Do?"

"Yeah."

"Well, later then. Cocktails, say, at the Oceanside?"

Iggy hesitated. It was going to be impossible to hide.

"Well, if you don't want to just say so." Heap looked hurt. It was a stupid sight.

"No, it's not that."

"Well, what then?"

"Okay, Heap," he sighed, "let's have a drink at the Oceanside about five-thirty, say?"

"Great!" Heap yelled and slapped Iggy on the back of the same shoulder he had punched moments before.

"Ow! Please don't do that. It hurts when you hit me. Doesn't anyone else ever tell you that?" He already regretted making the date and decided he wouldn't show up.

Heap laughed heartily. "See ya later, little guy. You can give me all your news and we'll have ourselves a real good time." He winked and waved as he went galumphing off down the street.

Heap Huggins was an American. Iggy first met him in 1969 when they were both barely out of their teens. He thought about that time in his life often. It had been easier to connect with people back then, with the drugs and temporary tolerance of one's fellow man. People bandied about the idea of trust for a while and recklessly gave themselves away. Far-fetched dreams had attached people to one another.

Iggy changed his mind. He would meet Heap after all. Letting those people go might mean that that time was insignificant. Iggy supposed it was, in the grand scheme of things, but not within the narrow parameters that defined his own life. Heap hadn't figured largely but had been on the periphery of the friends that Iggy ran with, friends like Iris. He knew that his memories were selective and romanticized, but whose weren't?

Heap loved Mexico. Iggy could remember him walking around singing that old Nilsson song, the one about "goin' where the weather suits my clothes." Heap's clothes must have been well-suited to Mexico because he never left.

Iggy walked around town for a bit and then headed to

the beach, where the beauty of the place astounded him one more time. He had always been drawn to water; at home he lived near the river and during the summer months he went out to the lakes as often as he could. But whenever he saw the ocean, especially in a warm climate where he could enter it, he felt like he was well and truly home. He rolled up his pant legs and walked along the shoreline, stopping now and then to rest and feel the sun. The tension began to leave him and he dozed against a smooth high rock.

Iggy dreamed that no one could see him. He walked among people he knew and they looked right through him. It was fun at first, he could eavesdrop, but everything he heard hurt his feelings. No one liked him, not even the people he loved. Everything they said was true, so even if he had been able to defend himself he wouldn't have known what to say.

He awoke with a clear sad head. A strange thought came to him and accompanied him to the bank. He thought if there was no one around to tell him who he was he'd swear he was someone else.

He sought out the biggest, most official-looking bank. It was stupid and dangerous for him to be carrying all that money, especially if he was going to be taking catnaps on deserted stretches of beach. It was his first visit to a Mexican bank and he was pleased to see it looked much like any bank back home, except it was smaller and warmer. Cool gusts from the fans made him shiver. He rented a safety deposit box and put the bulk of his fortune inside. There were as many keys and locked doors as there were back home but it didn't feel safe. What if this prim bank-worker's boyfriend was a much-feared bandito? Iggy pictured her late at night, laughter on her red lips, as she guided dangerous men to the small box that held his ill-gotten gains. There would be no record of the filthy money that was supposed to set him free.

Switzerland, then Scotland. He would get some advice from a well-positioned bank official who wouldn't ask him awkward questions. Just like the Switzerland in the movies.

It was four o'clock. Iggy scouted out a grocery store, where he bought some fruit and snack foods to take back to his room. In the lobby of the hotel he found a *Globe and Mail* only two days old. Canadians were about; he hoped he didn't know them.

Back in his room he showered again and lay down on the bed to worry. It was time to find Heap. He put on another clean shirt, ecru this time; it was kinder to his face than the stark white.

The boardwalk was teeming with people even in the off-season. There was so much to look at, so many beautiful brown bodies. The place stirred him as it always did; he wanted all the women he saw.

Heap was waiting. He had the best table in the house, by an open window. There was a view of the water that would include a sunset if they sat there long enough. Closer in, right outside and slightly below, was the same boardwalk Iggy walked in on.

Heap stood up and waved, shouting his name. The place was packed. Iggy weaved his way through the tables and sat down in the one empty chair.

"Hey, Igster, I didn't think you were gonna make it. Honey, this is Iggy Strand, the guy I was telling you about."

Honey was a lush-looking blonde woman who couldn't have been more than twenty. She wore a great deal of makeup and a peasant-style blouse that enhanced her smooth full breasts. Iggy wanted to press his face into the softness offered there but he forced himself not to stare. She reminded him of a sexy cartoon character, like a blonde Betty Boop, or a shorter rounder Jessica Rabbit with an unfortunate voice.

She offered Iggy a soft hand and said, "Pleased to meet you, I'm sure." It was a terrible sound, it cancelled out everything about her that was fantastic. Iggy was relieved, he didn't have to want her anymore.

Heap said, "Isn't she great?"

Iggy took her hand and said, "Sorry, I didn't catch your name."

"Honey!" Heap bellowed. He was still on his feet. "That's her real name. Honest! Show him your birth certificate, Honey." He leaned over and squeezed her and the most amazing sound came out. It was laughter, but Iggy wasn't sure at first because he thought it was connected to Heap's squeeze. She breathed in in a sort of gasp and then made wet snuffling sounds combined with a little squeal in her throat as she released the air. It was embarrassing to Iggy as it was very loud.

"No, no. I believe you," he shouted above the din, holding his hands up against any further knowledge of Honey.

"Well that's good." She smiled up at him the way some women do. They lower their heads so it becomes necessary for them to look up at whomever they're trying to impress. Iggy was tired of that particular affectation.

Heap hollered for service and finally sat down. The waiter took his time and Iggy didn't blame him. He probably knew Heap and didn't like him. Honey did like him and therefore was a puzzler to Iggy.

When the waiter finally came Iggy ordered Jack Daniels neat and was extra polite. Heap was drinking beer and Honey green Chartreuse. She must want to get swacked quickly, thought Iggy, or else not be familiar with the stuff. He bought them another round and they were soon settled in around their drinks.

"So, Honey, are you on vacation?" Iggy asked, after a giant swallow of the smoky elixir.

"Oh no, Sweetie. I work down the beach at the Pink Lady."

There goes my not familiar with Chartreuse theory, thought Iggy. He began plotting his getaway, he didn't want her to call him Sweetie anymore.

"My Honey-bunch is a cocktail waitress extraordinaire," piped up Heap. "That's how we met. She waited on me one night and we never looked back. Did we, Cutie-pie?"

Honey gave a quiet snort. "No, Heap darlin'." She looked at her watch. "I have to run, fellas. Iris'll kill me if I'm late."

Heap's face darkened. "Do you have to go home first?"

"Yeah, just to get changed. It was swell meeting you, Iggy. Heap's real excited that you're here. Drop into the Lady sometime and I'll spot you a drink."

"Sure, yeah, okay."

"See ya later, Heap honey." She kissed him wetly on his lips while she looked at Iggy, and then disappeared into the crowd.

"Iris who?" Iggy said.

Heap's face showed that he was lost in some dark thought till he heard Iggy shouting "Iris fucking who?" loudly enough for people at surrounding tables to go quiet and stare at him hopefully.

"Geez, Ig. Keep it down. We don't wanna get tossed out."

"Heap, I'm asking you a question. Is it Iris? Is she here?" He had finished his drink and was sitting flat and tense as an ironing board, leaning into Heap's answer.

"Oh yeah. You and old Iris. I forgot. Yeah, it's her. Do you wanna go see her?"

"Yes. No. I mean, yes, of course I'll see her but not right now. Look, Heap. I've got to go." He was on his feet.

"What! You just got here. Let me at least buy you a drink."

"I'm sorry, Heap. I really have to go. I'll be in touch." Iggy tried to sound friendly, gave Heap's shoulder a feeble punch.

"You don't know where I live," Heap sulked.

"Where do you live, Heap?" Iggy repressed his agitation as best he could. He didn't want to scatter himself all over a seedy bar.

"Up the hill a piece. Here, I'll give you the address."

"Okay, Heap, I'll see you." He saw Heap's expression and felt a surge of tenderness for the goofy guy who had presented him so suddenly with this new possibility. "Honest, I will."

The sea air was fresh and fragrant after the closeness of the bar. Iggy breathed deeply and walked till he felt better.

Oh! I have slipped the surly bonds of earth
And danced the skies on laughter-silvered wings.

The words came to him from somewhere but he couldn't remember who wrote them or when or why. They reminded him of Iris, the way she had been. He hadn't wanted to hear Heap talk about her, he didn't want her sullied by lummox words. When Iggy looked back, he saw her as a shining star; they had brought out the magic in each other. For a time.

Sometimes he was afraid he would forget her, not her really, but the way he had felt, the way they had felt together. So he would think about her face, her eyes, and try to bring back the joy, but what always came to him were the words she spoke the last time he saw her: "This is the best thing, Iggy. If I know you're in the world I'll be okay."

He had tried to understand that being enough for anyone and couldn't. It was like, if she had everything, it wasn't enough, so it was better not to have anything at all. An empty, sad philosophy.

So he had taken her small brown hands and held them as he looked into her saddened eyes. He meant to carry those eyes with him, and to make a safe place for her deep inside himself, so that what she believed would be true.

Chapter Four

Honey stopped at the house to change before work. She hoped Ernest would be busy in his greenhouse, or asleep, or anything that meant he wouldn't bother her.

She thought about Heap and wondered if he could help her. He said he loved her. Maybe that meant he would drive her so far away she would never be found. Ernest would stop looking for her and use someone else. Then she would have to lose Heap, which would be nothing compared to Ernest. Ernest was rich. He bought people and didn't let them go if he wasn't ready. Heap just loved her. If she said the right words to hurt him enough he would leave her alone.

She hated Ernest's bony hands and his dead-bird eyes. She hated his voice and the smell of him even before he got started on her.

When she stepped out of the shower he was waiting in the doorway.

"Good timing, little one. I'm ready for you." He held out his liver-spotted hands and she knew she had to move towards him.

"Don't bother with a towel. Come." He pinched her nipples with a strength that belied his frail-looking body, and watched her face for any sign of pain, but she smiled at him as though he were a beloved child and her nipples grew hard against the icy fingers. He took her to the glass doors that led to the patio behind the house.

"Outside?" Honey hesitated.

He prodded her forward. The yard was fenced on all sides but was within view of residents living further up the hill. There was a glass coffee table that sat close to the ground. Ernest had ordered Tomas to set it up in the yard. Honey lay on her back and inched her naked self underneath it while Ernest removed his clothes. She spread her legs and put her hands behind her head.

"Wider, dear. Open your mouth and look at me please."

At least one pair of eyes was fixed on this scene as Ernest climbed up on the table, squatted over her, and, as he held tightly to the withered cheeks of his own arse, pushed a steaming pile of shit out onto Honey's face.

She showered again. When she left for work Ernest was in his greenhouse and Tomas was on the patio cleaning up a putrid stinking mess. No one seeing his face would have been able to deduce anything from it. He had worked for Ernest long enough to know it was unwise to express himself within his master's sphere.

The sharp report of Ernest's handgun rang out that evening and the old man's brains splattered against the greenhouse glass that housed so many living breathing things.

Chapter Five
North

Audrey took the long way to the coffee shop, down the drive and underneath the bridge. It was sheltered and wild there, and there was always evidence of some kind: a lemon gin bottle, those old-fashioned condoms that looked like gloves for tiny tree people with long arms, a ratty old blanket. Once, an actual human being was there and he chose Audrey as the lucky gal to watch him as he reached his lonesome ecstasy. With no choice (his timing was right on) she obliged him briefly before stepping up her gait. No such treat today, however. She climbed up the grassy expanse to her favourite restaurant, where she bought a large coffee and a *Globe and Mail* to spread around her on the riverbank. The day was warm and golden; the river shone and there was a tree to lean against.

It seemed like she was always mad at her sister for one reason or another. Her most recent complaint (not counting this morning's fiasco) was the way Lillian cancelled out on her continually and at the last minute, not realizing or caring about the inconvenience. Again and again, Audrey would get organized for a lunch or a walk or a drive. And then, as she was heading out the door the phone would ring and her sister would be on the line, lying about the reason she couldn't be there. She would make something up, complicated to make it seem real so Audrey couldn't take issue with it. And if she did take issue there would be a fight.

"Would I make something like that up?" Lillian would shout.

"Yes," Audrey would reply.

Then more harsh words and the inevitable slamming down of the phone. Or Lillian wouldn't even call, so Audrey would be left dangling and furious. Or she would be three hours late, and say, "I'm sorry, something came up. Things do come up, you know," as though things didn't come up in Audrey's life. So Audrey had quit. She needed a break from the letdowns.

The newspaper seemed boring. Everything was old, rehashed—even the book reviews. Marilyn Monroe and backlashes. Audrey stared at the river, zoning out. She fell asleep for the third time that day and was wakened for the second time by her sister.

Lillian had taken her spot against the tree and was sucking on the long neck of a bottle of rotgut. There was a wine stain down the front of her tee shirt.

"Shit," was Audrey's response.

"Shit-eatin'," replied Lillian.

"Shit-eatin' dog-fuckin'—"

"Shit-eatin' dog-fuckin' prick-su—"

"Yeah, yeah. Forget it. I'm not talking to you." Audrey spat it out. Their game of dirty word progressions was something they had played since before they were teenagers. It was something they could really get together on, but Audrey was in no mood.

"What a shame. That conversation was goin' some-where." Lillian went back to her bottle.

"What's going on with you? Why did you run off?"

"I thought you weren't talkin' to me." Lillian had a little smile on her face that infuriated Audrey.

"How did you know to find me here?"

"I didn't. I just happened upon you."

"Look, Lillian, some stuff has happened, stuff I don't want any part of." What if the lying bitch didn't know about Iggy? Audrey thought. What if it hadn't been Lily who phoned the cops?

"Yeah, I know. Audrey, I have to tell you something." She sat down clumsily and spilled wine onto her bare arm. She began licking it off.

"Jesus." Audrey sidled away a little. "You better fuckin' have something to tell me. Where'd you get that wine?"

"At the liquor store."

"With what?"

"I borrowed some money from your cookie jar. I'll pay you back, honest."

"Well, thank you. Thank you very much. Thank you for using the opportunity of being alone in my home to steal from me. Get the fuck out of my sight, Lillian. Oh, and by the way, the cops are looking for you." Audrey was trying to gather her stuff together to get away. "God, I hate you," she muttered.

"Audrey, please."

"Please what?" she shrieked as she whirled around to face her sister. She saw that there were tears running down Lillian's face, many tears, although her face remained calm and unscrunched. Audrey felt her heart being squeezed by the haunted grey eyes. How could she blame those eyes? There was a lull in the traffic going over the bridge. The wind gently lifted Lillian's fine hair away from her face.

"There's a dead guy over at Iggy's place."

Chapter Six

Audrey sat at her kitchen table thinking about a dead stranger. Lillian sat across from her, unrefreshed from a shower and a lie-down, in a state of confused panic, her protective layer of shock worn off. Audrey looked at her closely. There were no answers on her cloudy face or in the movements of her shaky hands.

Frank was nowhere. Audrey left a message at the police station and then scribbled out a note which she sealed in an envelope. She took the phone off the hook, locked Lillian in the house and stepped next door.

Arthur was mucking around in his flower beds, preparing them for planting; she looked back at her own barren dirt patches. He smiled as she approached.

"Hello, Audrey dear. How are you?" He stood slowly, removing his peat-covered gloves. He needed time for the smallest of physical efforts. A thirty-year-old accident had left him with an injury to his right shinbone that resulted in one leg being inches shorter than the other. His right shoe had a four-and-a-half-inch lift that evened him out and made walking more comfortable.

Arthur lost both parents in the accident as well as his younger sister and his dog, Yellow. A wind had come up on the lake and his father shouted, "Batten down the hatches!" That was the last thing Arthur heard him say. The man whose vessel sailed clear through the Pointes' boat was alone, with no one to batten his hatches down for him, so he had been doing it himself and had, therefore, spread himself too thin.

That event whipped the rug out from under Arthur at fifteen, when he was about to score with Darlene Summerfield. Yellow was the one he mourned. People had comforted him and he had confided willingly. He hoped someone would have something wise to say about the lack of feeling he had for his family. He had never questioned it when they were alive because he hadn't known. Grown-ups patted his hand and told him they were sure his grief was on a back burner and it would come to the forefront when he was ready. Friends shuffled their feet, not knowing what kinds of answers to give. And Darlene went ahead and did it with his best friend, Pierce Rayburn. He couldn't get over that. He couldn't get over Yellow, and he couldn't get over Pierce having sex with Darlene when he knew that Arthur was almost there.

Audrey answered, "Hi Arthur. Well, I've had better days. I'm hoping that you'll do a favour for me."

"Anything." He whacked his gloves against his thigh, making a small peat cloud in the air around him.

"I hate to bother you with this, but, well, are you going to be home for the next few hours?"

"I am so." (In the small town where Arthur spent his first fifteen years, folks had the habit of adding 'so' to the end of certain sentences when Prairie people least expected it. It was the only noticeable Ontarioism that he hung onto.)

"Well, I'm going out and there's a chance a policeman will be coming to my house. I've written a letter for him and it's real important. Could I leave it with you and put a note on my door telling him that? I just don't want to leave the actual letter on my door."

"No problemo."

"Thanks a real lot, Arthur."

"Don't worry now. I'll see he gets it if he comes by."

"He won't be wearing a uniform, just regular clothes. It's quite possible he won't even show up, but if he does . . ."

"Off you go, Audrey."

After Audrey left, Arthur decided on a rooftop break. He had rigged up a sitting spot for himself on top of his veranda that he could get to from a second-storey window. It gave him a marvellous view, a real sense of the lay of the land on any particular day.

He loved the prairies and the way they made him feel. He had arrived by train on a cloudless day all those years ago. The wind had moved through the tall grass in a way that made him feel like he'd felt with his thoughts of Darlene, before, when it was still possible. The nervousness and pain were missing and that made it a bit different, better in some ways, and nowhere near as grand in others. The wide blue sky filled him with hope and peace. His thoughts reached farther here; there were no barriers.

People said it was the kind of city where you had to be born and raised to love it truly, and to get why people stayed. Arthur disagreed. He loved it immediately and deeply and always. He had come to stay with his aunt Joan and uncle Len, who was his mother's brother. They were considerably older than his parents and had no children, which was fine with Arthur. He didn't mind leaving the small town where he had grown up; the Pierce-Darlene liaison contributed to his desire to get away. Also, he thought the huge lift on his shoe would be less conspicuous in the city.

It had taken him a while to learn to walk again and he became very good at sitting and reclining. He became a new person. With the drastic changes in his life, the forced new circumstances, large parts of his old self were left behind, somewhere between "Batten down the hatches!" and the unexpected joy he felt at the flatness of his new home.

And as for the grief, simmering away on the back burner, so far he hadn't seen it. It made him wonder a bit about himself, what he saw as his emotional shortcomings, but he felt many things deeply, perhaps even love for one or two people, so tried not to worry about that puzzling blank area in his life.

He looked towards the river now, shining in the distance, and let it take him away. He didn't sleep but went somewhere good. It was easy for him to feel that he was that shine atop the swift current of waters, he was the shine and it surrounded him too, till there was nothing else.

When Audrey returned home she found Lillian lying on the couch. Her cat had stretched out across her sister's chest and buried his little face in the crook of her neck. They both had their eyes closed but neither slept.

"Time to get up!"

Lillian opened her eyes and kissed the tabby, who pretended that Audrey hadn't spoken.

"Let's go," Audrey said.

"What?" Lillian gently removed Craig from her neck and sat up hugging him to her chest.

Audrey had lent her a shirt and a pair of cotton pants, not two of her favourite items of clothing, but they looked okay and at least didn't have wine slopped down the front.

"Let's go."

"Where're we goin'?" Lillian was still quivery and dopey as she got to her feet.

"Come on. We'll talk on the way." Audrey replaced the phone and pushed her sister out the door. She locked it and attached the note.

Once on the road she explained, "We're going to the police station."

"What?"

"We have to, Lily; we have no choice. Frank'll turn up soon and make things easier for us."

"Why, why do we have to? We didn't do anything; I didn't do anything. Oh God, where's Iggy?" Lillian flopped about in the front seat as the small wagon bumped crazily over the spring roads.

Audrey turned on the radio. "Boys of Summer." The familiar feeling that washed over her at the sound of Don Henley's voice hurt her; she wished it would go away.

"Lily, fasten your seatbelt please." Audrey swung wide onto the main thoroughfare. "A dead man was found in your and Iggy's apartment. We have to present you to the police because they want to see you. If you avoid them you appear guilty of something. Not only that, but the last time I talked to a cop he thought the dead guy was Ignatius Strand. They may all still think that. We've got to help; it's our duty as people."

"I think I'm gonna barf." Lillian's face was white and her lips had disappeared into the paleness. "Audrey, stop the car. I'm gonna barf!"

Audrey pulled over to the curb lane, put on her flashers, and stopped the car. She cut somebody off in the process and a horn exploded in her head.

"Fuck you, mister!" she shrieked over her shoulder as she raced around to Lillian's side of the vehicle.

Lillian spewed a mess of wine and coffee all over the curb, and managed to get a little on Audrey's clothes and car. When she was breathing normally and looking a little better Audrey drove to a gas station, where Lillian splashed water on her face. Audrey bought her a Coke to burn out the inside of her mouth and throat.

"All set?" They were back in the car and Audrey was determined to get the thing done. They pulled into the parking lot at the police station. She handed her sister a comb and watched her run it through her thin hair. Did she know what she looked like? She used to be vain, now she looked ready to die. Not yet Lily, please, not just yet. Audrey went off on one of her tangents: if Lily could just be okay, I'll be nicer, I'll treat her better, I'll act like I have a family, I'll invite relatives over for Thanksgiving dinner and we'll play games after supper. Yeah, right.

"Do you really not know where he is?" she asked.

Lily shook her head. Their eyes met for a moment and Lily smiled a small hopeless smile that filled Audrey's eyes suddenly with tears that just as quickly vanished. She put her arm around her sister as they plodded across the empty white parking lot. The need she felt was a bit confusing to her; she couldn't quite find its place in the neat compartments of her mind.

The huge policeman at the front desk informed them that Inspector Foote wasn't there and wouldn't be back that day.

"Did he say why?" Audrey asked.

"No ma'am."

"Is there a phone I could use?"

He pointed his chin at a pay phone across the room. She tried Frank again at home and talked to the babysitter. Mr. Foote was out with Mrs. Foote. She didn't know when he'd be back. Audrey left a message, holding on to Lillian by her shirt-tail all the while.

"He's out somewhere with Denise, for Christ's sake. Bitch. Whore!"

Lillian made a quiet sound.

"What was that?" Audrey asked. "Was that a laugh? Are you laughing?"

"Yeah. So, punch me out." Lillian wrested her wadded-up crinkled shirt-tail from Audrey's grasp.

"What's so freaking funny?"

"It's just kind of a riot that you still hate Denise."

"Don't be stupid. I don't hate her. I don't even know the feeble witch."

Lillian's eyes were closed. "Audrey, please don't talk so loud all the time."

"Sorry."

"I saw Denise Foote at the liquor store this morning," said Lillian.

"You're kidding!"

"No. Can we sit down?"

"What was she doing? How did she look?"

"She looked great but she was hosed. And she was buying tiny bottles of Silent Sam." Lillian swayed a little as she talked.

"Really? Is she a drunk?"

"I don't know. How would I know?"

"Wow. Maybe Frank's wife's a drunk."

"Maybe. So what?"

They walked back to the officer at the desk. He clutched a half-eaten Peanut Butter Cup in his hand. Audrey began, "Mr. Foote's partner, Fred . . ."

"That'd be Detective Sergeant Freddy Staples."

Audrey averted her eyes from the mess in his mouth.

"Would it be possible to speak to him?" She focussed on the little gold chain on his desk lamp.

"With regards ta what?" He swallowed what he was working on but took another bite. Audrey glanced at Lillian, who looked as though she might be sick again.

"Just a minute, please." She led her sister over to a small couch and sat her down. "Are you going to be okay?"

"I could sure use a drink."

"Don't be such an idiot!" Audrey hissed.

"No, no. I mean like water. I'm just so dry, and I taste like barf. That Coke hurt too much to swallow." She held onto her throat.

"Oh. Okay." Audrey looked at the big policeman, who was staring at them, his mouth busy around a new chocolate bar. "Stay here." She walked back to the desk and spoke to his neck. "Is there a coffee shop?"

"Down the hall, first right, first left. Is your pal all right? She don't look so good from where I'm sittin'."

"She'll be fine. I just need to get her something to drink. Thanks."

Audrey bought two apple juices in cans and bumped into Fred in the cashier's lineup. It took her a moment to recognize his short dark hair with its fringe of elfin bangs and the tidy beard. His eyes were round and surprised-looking and this was emphasized by the circular frames of his glasses. His lips formed a cute circle around his mouth and Audrey couldn't help but think if he were turned upside down he would look about the same.

She greeted him with a handshake. "Hi Fred. Audrey

Laird. We weren't introduced this morning. Could I talk to you for a few minutes?"

"Sure thing, Ms. Laird. Just let me get this paid for." He hung onto what looked to be a lime milkshake.

Fred found a tiny room with a couple of chairs and a table. Audrey was anxious to get back to Lillian. She explained that her sister had some information. Fred was excited. He wanted to do things correctly.

"Okay. I'll let you get back to your sister and I'll go see if Superintendent Flagston wants to join us while I take a statement. I'm sorry Frank isn't here."

"Where is he?"

"Uh, trouble of some kind at home." Fred took a drink of his shake and was left with a pale green line above his lips.

Audrey stared at it, realizing that he didn't have a real moustache, just the lime one with the beard beneath. "At home? Nothing serious, I hope?"

"I don't really know the ins and outs." He licked his upper lip and the pastel moustache disappeared. "I just got the word that Frank wouldn't be back today. It's a heck of a day for him to book off, so I assume he's got good reason."

"Oh dear."

"Yeah. Okay, I'll see you in a few minutes."

Audrey hightailed it back to the lobby. She liked Fred more than she thought she was going to and felt as though things were going okay, except for whatever was happening with Frank. And the fact that Lillian was nowhere to be seen.

She looked around frantically, ran out the front door, back in, and shouted at the officer behind the desk, "Where did she go?"

"Who?"

"My sister. I left her sitting there." Audrey pointed at the empty couch.

"Beats me." The officer was intent on undoing the wrapping on a brand new chocolate bar.

"Oh God. I don't think I can stand any more of this. Look, I have to find her. If Fred comes—"

"Ms. Laird?" She turned to see Fred and a scruffy-looking man he introduced as Superintendent Flagston.

"Lily's gone."

The superintendent put a firm hand on her forearm to stop her as she headed once more for the doors.

Ed Flagston fixed his tired eyes on the fat man behind the desk. "Do you know anything about this, Weizner?"

"No, sir." Weizner tried to look alert and interested. Audrey wanted to see him get reamed.

"No, I thought not." Flagston sighed and led Audrey over to the ratty old couch. "I'm going to send a couple of cars out. Do you have any suggestions, Ms. Laird?"

"I don't know, just hurry. She couldn't be far." Audrey looked at her watch and was on her feet again. Why were they sitting here wasting time? "It's been less than fifteen minutes since I left her sitting here, and she wasn't feeling well. I can't believe she had the wherewithal to take off." She turned back to Weizner. "Are you sure you didn't see anything? Did anyone come in and talk to her?"

Weizner puffed his cheeks out with air and shook his head. Flagston sighed again. "Give Fred a description of your sister and he'll get two teams out looking for her."

Audrey did as she was told.

"We'll be in my office, Fred. Join us there as soon as you can."

Audrey said, "No, I have to go too."

Flagston propelled her down the hallway. "I think we'd better get a statement from you to tide us over till we find your sister."

"Oh dear."

"If it's not too much trouble, that is."

"Oh, I'm sorry. Of course, lead the way."

"In here Ms. Laird."

"Please, it's Audrey."

"Okay Audrey." His office was a mess. He lit an Export "A" and offered her one. She accepted. It was her brand. She just hadn't had one in nineteen years. He held a match to her cigarette, she inhaled once and fainted.

Chapter Seven
South

Iggy walked by the water's edge toward the Pink Lady. He wondered how Iris had weathered the years. The first time he'd seen her was on the same stretch of beach he walked on now. She had worn a polka-dotted bikini and laughed insanely with a group of friends. Her blonde hair fell thick and wavy down her back. She sat up very straight and Iggy was smitten before she even turned around. He watched her, willing her to look at him. She did and her smile made his heart leap up. He sat down close enough to smell the coconut oil she had smoothed on her long brown thighs; he wanted to lick them.

"Where are you from?" he had asked.

"Canada."

"Me too! Whereabouts?"

"North Ontario. How about you? Where're you from?"

He remembered "Something in the Way She Moves" coming out of the little portable stereo. The music described how he felt, over and over, and she always smiled just when he needed to know that she knew it too. They smoked cigarettes and drank from a wineskin till evening came and goose bumps showed up on her tanned skin.

They noticed then that Heap was buried up to his neck in the sand and couldn't get out. He was shouting at the rest of their companions, who were walking away down the beach, "Hey, you assholes, get me out of here. Hey! Come back!"

Iris and Iggy started to laugh and didn't stop till they had dug him out and sent him on his way.

When they left the beach they looked over their shoulders at the way the ocean met the sky as the day waned. And they came back before dawn, to watch the sun come up on the other side of things. It seemed important not to miss that. He remembered those feelings now but couldn't imagine actually having anything like them ever again.

Iris arrived late for work, out of breath and full of apologies. The place was filling up the way it had the night before. The way things were going, she figured she'd be able to close the restaurant for a couple of months in future off-seasons, maybe even the next year. She looked forward to spending less time on her feet. She seated people as they arrived, kept an eye on the whole of it.

The restaurant looked just the way she had pictured it four years earlier—peach tablecloths and flowers. Ernest grew them for her. She had liked the flowers once but they had come to remind her of garbage. The sickly sweet smell of his freesias turned her stomach more readily than the overflowing dustbins outside the kitchen door.

The bar was less formal, no cloth or flowers there. Some of the tables were right next to the beach and the whole open west side was an entrance. Iris' open-air bar was a welcoming sight to beach walkers and boaters cruising for a place to stop.

Her thick blonde hair was touched with grey. Iggy stared as she bent her head to the list of reservations. He recognized the combination of hair and posture.

"Hello, Iris."

She raised her head slowly to the familiar voice, not quite placing it, but knowing it was a good thing.

"Iggy? Is it really you?"

He smiled. "The one and only."

"Oh my. Oh, this is grand." She came from behind her little desk and hugged him to her. She felt small and stiff to Iggy. In his memory she was rounded, cushiony and soft. But she seemed okay, she was safe.

"Let me look at you." She had her hands on his shoulders, holding him at arm's length. "Oh, Iggy, I just can't say how glad I am." Her eyes were filled with tears but her small face shone and Iggy basked; he felt warm clear through.

He felt a surge of hope but knew that he'd best let it go. There was no reason for him to think it would be any easier after more than twenty years. There was no longer even incautious youth to aid him in his blundering. He was so much more afraid of making a fool of himself as he grew older. It was so easy to do, and he cringed at thoughts of how thoroughly he could embarrass himself.

He felt a vague longing. The past showing itself and being so different from his present, from what he had become, sent waves of sadness through him. It seemed too hard to learn to work with what that past had become in Iris. Iggy wanted what wasn't possible, to go back and try again. He felt lazy and foolish and glad.

"Let's sit down. Have dinner with me?" Iris pulled him towards a table.

"Of course," Iggy shouted happily.

"Good. We've got prawns that were in the ocean less than an hour ago."

"Perfect."

They beamed at each other.

"Let me just go and speak to the cook. I'll be right back. What'll you have to drink?"

"Do you make a good small margarita?"

"We do."

"Okay, one of those please. Will you join me?"

She nodded, smiling, and Iggy watched as she moved off towards the kitchen. People were seating themselves and Iris stopped to help organize them. She wore a long diaphanous dress that gently protected her lean brown legs. Overtop, a pale blue cotton shirt was open and knotted at her waist. On her feet were sturdy Mexican sandals. As she pushed open the door to the kitchen she looked over her shoulder and smiled. Iggy felt blessed. He saw a strength and dignity about her, without any aloofness to ruin it. It was her spirit that was strong. Her tiny physical self looked like it would dissipate in a strong gust of wind.

He remembered their first days when they had searched so fervently with their eyes wide open, letting everything in and talking all night till they thought they had it figured. They were constantly amazed with each other, with themselves, with the world. They tried to be the types of people on whom nothing was lost.

"Iggy, I didn't know you were here."

The loud voice squealing in his ear sent a shock through his mid-section that started him shaking. "Jesus, Honey, you scared me!"

She laughed as she put the margaritas down in front of him. "Come sit at the bar and we can have a good old chat while I work."

"Thanks, but I'm having dinner with Iris. We're old friends." Iggy sounded to himself like he had a broom-handle stuck up his ass all the way to his head to keep him in place.

"Oh. Cool. I didn't know you knew Iris. Well, some other time." She brushed the table clear of non-existent crumbs, leaning over to give him a better view of her breasts. The move puzzled him. Did she want him, a skittery middle-aged drifter who had shown her nothing more than a strained politeness? Not so far-fetched if it was true she felt desire for Heap Huggins. Nah. More likely she was just getting off on herself and her redoubtable sexual power. She was young, maybe it was new to her and she couldn't get over it. Whatever it was, he was pretty sure it had nothing to do with him and was best left alone.

"Yeah, okay. Catch ya later." Iggy sipped his drink and willed his body into neutral. Honey walked away, bending from the waist partway across the room to pick up nothing and let Iggy know she wasn't wearing underwear. He wished she would stop doing things like that.

Iris returned, still smiling, with bowls of steaming mussels and a loaf of warm bread.

"Let's start with this."

Iggy ripped off an end of the loaf and dragged it through the broth to his mouth.

"Mmm. Wow, Iris. You're really in your element here. I remember this place from ages ago. Have you been here long?"

She explained how they had come to own the place.

"The money was all his so I was leery. But he was rich and I wasn't and I wanted the place so bad. I still feel pretty weird about it. Money scares me."

It got harder to chew the more Iris talked. "Money's scary stuff." Iggy didn't take any new bites, just worked on getting rid of what was already in his mouth.

Iris remembered how she had felt when Ernest placed the deed in her hands. They had just eaten dinner and the pasta sat like muck in her stomach. She felt she had been pushed, that her original idea was snatched away and made into something strange and bad, like his flowers.

She knew enough of him by then not to like him any-more. He ruined things, covered them with a film of grime, making nightmares of dreams and daily life. She wished she had known better than to want something as much as she wanted the restaurant. Now it was too late. The Pink Lady was tainted with his bloody money.

"I manage everything," she continued. "He does the flow-ers. That's it. It's doing okay. Pretty soon I'll be in the black." Iris' smile was forced.

She's trapped, Iggy thought.

"What about you, Iggy? What have you been doing for

the last twenty-five years? You look great. Whatever it was must have agreed with you."

"Oh, thanks. Well, it kept me on my toes, anyway," he smiled. He didn't want to talk about his years as a drug fiend and the endless deals that made him feel ashamed before her. "I've been back here a couple of times but I didn't know you were still here. If I hadn't run into Heap . . ."

"Yeah, Heap eh?" Iris fooled around with a small piece of bread, ignoring the mussels entirely. "I've gotten kind of used to him over the years. He's not such a bad guy. I guess I've actually been friends with him on a semi-regular basis longer than anyone else on earth. Weird, eh?" She almost took a bite but seemed to think better of it and returned the bread to her plate.

"Yeah, Heap. I should have been nicer to him. It's just he cuts so wide a swath and I have trouble with that. I'd rather just kind of slither through life."

Iris laughed. Iggy envied Heap's position as her friend. He felt that he himself was a good friend to no one, important to no one; nobody needed him even a little bit. If he died it would be okay with pretty well everyone; there would be no grieving for Ignatius Strand. There was Lillian, but she was too fucked over to need him in any real sort of way and he hadn't wanted her to anyway. He didn't know what the fuck he wanted. He just knew that for whatever reasons, he wasn't good friend material.

When Iris went off to see about wine, Iggy sought out the men's room. He walked through the bar, where he caught another sighting of Honey. She was leaning on the bar, her arms folded under her breasts crushing them against the thin cloth of her blouse. She stared at the man across from her. He was talking to the man next to him and as he talked he moved his fingers lightly against the skimpy material that contained Honey's breasts. Even from where Iggy stood he could see her nipples hard against the cloth. She looked up and her eyes were two burnt holes in her face. She saw him and winked, or anyway, she lowered one lid down over one black hole. Iggy couldn't believe that Iris didn't know. People were watching. Iggy lurched toward the washroom and avoided her on his way back.

"You do know that your cocktail waitress is a nymphomaniac."

Iggy had just finished the best prawns he had ever tasted, lightly grilled, very lightly seasoned, to perfection. Iris even ate one or two. The wine had gone down easily and they felt comfortable with each other.

Iris lowered her eyes with a blush and put her hands under the table on her lap. It was as though she had been caught smoking in the girls' room. "She's a very good waitress." She looked at Iggy. "I'm a little worried that Heap might be in for a real pummelling. I don't think he has any idea."

"He must have some Christly idea!"

She laughed, "Poor Iggy. You look so perplexed."

Chapter Eight
North

When Audrey awoke she was looking into Frank's eyes. She felt a loving warmth toward the three men whose faces hovered over her. If more faces appeared she would love them too. Audrey had these moments now and then, usually upon awakening. She thought of them as her religion.

Frank knelt beside her, holding her hand. "Audrey? Hi. You fainted but you're okay." He adjusted a man's raincoat that covered parts of her. Her feet were sticking out and hanging over the end of the too-short couch where she had ended up. "Do you think you can sit up?"

Fred produced a glass of water. She sat up on her elbow and took a sip. "Thanks, I'm sorry, what time is it?"

"Just a few minutes have gone by. You haven't missed anything."

"I guess it was the cigarette. I haven't really smoked in a while."

Frank looked up at Flagston, who shrugged. "I didn't know. How was I supposed to know?"

Frank smiled, "That'll teach ya. Have you eaten anything lately?"

Audrey had a vague recollection of a fine banana way back in her carefree early morning. She reminded herself to try to notice and appreciate more the days when nothing weird or troublesome happens. And there had been a fudgsicle that hadn't worked out. "No, I guess not."

"Fred, would you mind zipping off to the caf and getting a bowl of soup?" He turned to Audrey. "Is mushroom okay?"

"I love mushroom soup." She felt like she was five years old but was enjoying herself immensely. She sat right up. "Did you find Lillian?"

"No, but we will. Don't worry."

"Frank, are you okay? You're not supposed to be here."

"Don't worry about that either."

Frank sighed as he recalled the conversation between himself and Denise hours ago, before he dropped her off at the Chemical Withdrawal Unit. He hadn't been able to tell her he loved her. It had been so long since he had felt that love, he didn't know if it was still there under all the wretchedness and empty spaces of their life together. And he hadn't wanted to lie. He wished now that he had. It had never been her idea to go into the rehab before. Maybe it wasn't too late.

The soup made Audrey feel stronger. She sat at Ed Flagston's desk, amongst the dirty ashtrays and coffee mugs. The superintendent went home after Frank assured him he would stay to get Audrey's statement and pursue the Lillian angle. The police knew that the dead man was not Ignatius Strand but they didn't know who he was. They had Iggy's fingerprints on file so it didn't take long to determine who he wasn't.

Frank and Fred were variously leaning and sitting around the room, giving Audrey a chance to finish her soup.

Finally she spoke. "I should have been more careful; she disappeared once today already. But she was so sick, I just didn't figure on it."

Fred didn't write much down. And they didn't make Audrey look at the pictures of the dead man even though they had them there. They believed in her separateness from her sister. She gave them all she could.

When she paused Frank said, "I'm relieved to hear you tell it. You called this guy Iggy when I was at your house and I knew I had only used his full name, Ignatius Strand. It seemed weird that you would use that nickname if you had never heard of the guy."

"I hated not telling you everything, Frank. I don't even know now why I didn't."

"Don't worry."

"I figured I had probably messed up somewhere in our conversation. I'm not all that good at pulling the wool over people's eyes."

Frank crouched in the middle of the room in what looked to be a horribly uncomfortable position. His knees must be in better shape than mine, thought Audrey.

"It was just as I was leaving when you asked me what he was listening to on the headphones. Oh, and, according to that"—he pointed at the folder on the desk—"the guy was listening to *Machine Head*, Deep Purple. I guess he was an old-school heavy metal kinda dude."

"Dude?"

"Sorry."

Fred had started to feel that perhaps the interview was over. "I guess that's it then, Ms. Laird."

"Please, it's Audrey."

"Okay, Audrey. Unless there's something else you'd like to add just sign there at the bottom and we'll call it a statement."

Audrey signed and Fred said good night.

"Very dapper lad, your Fred."

"Yes, very trim," Frank grinned.

Audrey laughed and Frank stood up, stretched and suggested that they go and get some food.

"Where?"

"I don't know. Where would you like to go?"

"Hmm. Why don't we just go back to my house and I'll make us a sandwich. I don't want to not be there if Lily shows up again. Although I can't really picture it."

"What do you mean?"

"I don't know. I think she's gone." Audrey twirled a couple of times around the police superintendent's office. It wasn't a situation she was likely to be in again soon.

"Let's go." Frank herded her out into the clear May night. The city looked unreal to Audrey, as though it were a giant set, painted for a play. She wished she and Frank could step out of it and just be in the audience, holding hands, letting someone else figure out what was supposed to happen next.

Chapter Nine

Lillian wondered when it had happened that she was no longer part of anything. Endings can do that, suddenly set people adrift so easily when they thought they were on solid ground. It wasn't just Iggy. She knew she was lost long before that, knew that the fullness of life depended on connections, including the one to her self that was sometimes hard or impossible to reach or figure.

For so long she had lived only through her body till she saw it start to change and grew to hate it. That left nothing unless you counted family, which she didn't. She thought of her family as a controlled artificial environment like a sick greenhouse that nurtured a mutant seed and brought to fruition its fury and hopelessness.

Audrey said it was too much to expect that life have any meaning all on its own. People had to make up their own stuff, to plump it out. They had to put their own energy to work. That's what she had said. Audrey was so cheerful she made Lillian sick; that was why she hardly ever visited her.

Arthur had spoken to her about family and he had used the word forgiveness. She liked Arthur but he seemed almost like a different species, capable of things normal guys weren't, like forgiveness.

Everything Lillian saw enraged her and when she

lashed out she became so fierce she drove people away. She couldn't find anyone low enough to be her friend. On certain warm days she thought she would just start walking south, straight south to Miami or Mexico where she would find a beach filled with desperate characters. Maybe there she would find a person to talk to, someone who would be so nice to her that her words would come out soft and kind again. She knew that deep inside her, covered with all the years of her life, there was something good and light, worth saving. It was from a long time ago, before anything that she could remember.

Her left eye was twitching out of her head. If she could just get to that warm beach she was sure it would stop. Her luck would change there and her fear become something she could handle.

Chapter Ten
South

The sun had set and the clouds near the horizon made a spectacular display. They were moving about, making plans. Iggy sat on a bench in the sand a short way down the beach from the restaurant. He was waiting for Iris to close up.

She was still sad, he thought. She had always had a sense of melancholy about her that Iggy hadn't understood or felt able to penetrate; she hadn't let him. He'd needed reassurance which she wasn't always able to give. During his worst moments he'd felt that he didn't know her at all, that her innocence and guilelessness, her pure soul, her gentle self were a façade. But only when he wasn't with her.

He watched her now, walking slowly towards him, smiling at him as she held her skirt down against the wind, and he wondered how he could ever have thought such a thing.

They sat in silence for a while. A skinny dog hung around and Iggy gave its ears a good scratch. Iris was subdued. "About Honey—"

"You don't have to explain anything to me, Iris." The dog followed his hand and placed its small bony head under Iggy's fingers.

"No. I'd like to talk to you about her, unless you don't want me to."

"Talk away." Iggy smiled and threw his arms out wide

to make room for Iris' words. The dog leapt back at the sudden movement and scrambled away down the beach.

"Sorry!" Iggy shouted after it.

"Do you have a cigarette?"

He didn't, but walked down the beach a ways and bought two Camels from a waiter who stood smoking behind his workplace.

They lit up and the breeze whisked their smoke away before it had a chance to play around their faces.

"Ernest found her a couple of years ago when she was just barely into her teens."

"How Christly old is she now?"

"Sixteen. Just. Don't tell anyone, she'd kill me."

"Good Christ! Sixteen! I mean, it's not that she looks old, it's just that she's so, so . . ."

"Yeah. I know. Well anyway, she lived upstairs at the Oceanside, conducted her business there." Iris worked a hangnail so hard that Iggy had to sit on his hands. "I guess she's led a pretty weird life but you'd never know it talking to her, she's tough. But that worries me, there's gotta be stuff festering inside her and I get visions of *Sybil* sometimes and wonder if it'll all come out later in really twisted behaviour of some sort."

"Iris, her behaviour now is really twisted, don't you think? She's gonna cause a riot in there." Iggy looked back towards the bar and saw the mangy old dog standing off a ways, hopeful.

"Oh God, it is bad, isn't it? I haven't known what to say to her."

"Here, old fella!" Iggy called and the dog came bounding back. It moved awkwardly on its feet as though they weren't right in some way. "Where's Heap in all this?"

"He's trying to save her, I guess. He doesn't seem to see a lot but I guess that's just his way. I'm not sure he knows the whole score when it comes to Ernest either. Ernest . . ."

"What? Ernest what?" The dog closed his eyes and gave himself to the skinny man who made his ears feel good. "This old dog's got sore feet," Iggy said.

Iris continued, "He was a psychiatrist, you see, in England before he . . ."

"Before he what?"

"Let's not talk about Ernest. I hope you realize that you now own this dog."

"How did Ernest find Honey?"

"Well . . . ," Iris sighed, "he was drinking at the Oceanside and she came on to him. He didn't want to pay her, but that was the only thing stopping him."

She looked out at the disappearing ocean. The darkness moved in and the wind died down. The dog settled in around Iggy's feet and quiet water sounds were all they could hear.

Iggy wished he'd missed this glimpse of Ernest. What was this guy? He wasn't sure he wanted to find out. What he did want was for Iris to be okay, the way he had thought she was when he first saw her in the restaurant. He saw now that she had found someone to hurt her, the way he hadn't been able to. He wondered if he should have stayed and tried harder to be what she wanted him to be, out of love, to save her from the Ernests of the world.

He had wanted to be all things to her, anything she needed. And she was needy, and confounded by her own greed. The pleasure was never enough. He had tried to ask her what she wanted but she had just smiled a sick smile. "You're great. Don't worry so much."

One night as he gripped her hair in his fists, pounding into her again and again, her head hit the wall and he stopped, terrified that she might be hurt. She screamed "No!" and as he watched in horror she banged her head, over and over till her blood stained the wall above the bed. Tears streamed down her face and the smallest of smiles flickered, before dying there. He held her while she cried and she clung to him then. After that he had felt clumsy in his efforts to please her, had known he didn't have a hope.

"Were you and Ernest together, like partners, when he found her?" Iggy asked.

"Oh, Iggy. Please don't worry. I don't think I could bear it if you started worrying about me again." She put her hand on his and smiled into his troubled face. "Please. I went into this with my eyes open. I don't need more than what he can give me. I don't. And I feel okay, quite free really, now that he doesn't want me sexually anymore. Well, not free maybe, but left alone, which actually has come to be what I want the most."

She stopped, as though she had said too much.

"Why do you stay?"

She kept on as though he hadn't spoken. "He's pretty weird and it got worse for me when Honey entered the picture, but my part in that didn't last long. And I figured it was worth it."

"Why? What was worth it? Why do you stay with him?" Iggy could hear the shrillness in his voice. He tried to comfort himself with knowing that the hands of the pervert with whom Iris chose to live no longer wounded her soft flesh.

"He's rich," she said simply.

Iggy said nothing. Iris had been living for well over forty years. She was established as a person with layers and layers that he knew nothing about. He couldn't presume to impose or even judge.

It came to him that he knew nothing. Any ideas he had about existence and what life could be were simply that: ideas, his own stupid ideas. He had nothing to base anything on but his own life of haphazard experience. As soon as he saw clearly into someone else's world he was let down, and not just by what he saw, but by himself for being disappointed, for having naive expectations. He was ashamed of his disappointment. Iris shouldn't have to know about it. Despair crept in and settled, familiar as his face. Despair and a flea-bitten dog.

When he spoke it came out a monotone. "What do you mean it got worse when Honey entered the picture?"

"I mean when Ernest brought her home and into our bed."

A few yards away on another bench two tiny old men sat smoking, holding court before twelve doting seagulls. Iggy hadn't seen them come.

Switzerland and Scotland seemed far out of reach; he wanted only to lie down and rest.

Chapter Eleven

"I don't want to go back to Ernest and Iris'."

"Okay. Great. What do you want to do?" Heap had picked Honey up at the end of her shift.

"I mean, I don't want to go back ever." Honey pushed her blouse down so that her breasts were free.

Heap groaned and reached over to touch the soft mounds with his huge brown hand. He pulled over and stopped the van.

"Fuck me, Heap." Honey's skirt was up around her waist and she swung her legs onto his shoulders.

"Christ, Honey, right here?" Passers-by could see what was going on but she didn't care. Heap did, but not enough to argue; he would do anything rather than risk losing her. A normal life was what he wanted. He had grave doubts but kept on trying.

Honey made herself come. The shuddering paroxysm left her limp and briefly spent. Heap lifted her into the back of the van where there were curtains to keep out the lascivious stares of the people on the street. He never felt farther away from Honey than when they had sex. It didn't make it any less exciting, but it was something she did on her own, without him. She never looked at him, although she did talk, endlessly, with that horrible honking voice. He wished she'd shut up.

She was on her knees. Her breasts leapt and bobbled in his face as she made a shimmying motion with her shoulders.

"Do you like to see my tits jiggle, Heap?" Her eyes were closed.

He flushed with embarrassment, stood and pressed the hardness of his cock against the smooth skin of her face. He hated her words but beneath them he sensed her need for something he could give her. If he just knew what it was, if he could find it and give it to her, she would be okay.

"Fuck my mouth, Heap. Fuck my throat. I need your cock inside me."

"Shut up," he whispered as he entered her and began to slap himself hard against her pretty face.

Chapter Twelve
North

They ate grilled cheese sandwiches and Frank drank the beer Audrey had been saving. The lamplight gave the porch a cosy glow, an island of light in the warm black night. They heard the voices of night walkers passing. Audrey was on the couch and Frank on the stool. His hair was longish at the back, touching the collar of his shirt in a way that effected a feeling of tightness in Audrey's stomach.

She set aside her sandwich. "I'm sorry I held back on you this morning. It must have made you suspicious."

"Not suspicious really, just kind of sad. I didn't want you on the other side of anything from me."

"Oh." It was a strangled sound and Audrey tried changing it into a cough.

"I don't blame you for trying to protect your sister."

Audrey had no idea whether Frank was feeling the same sorts of things she was. How was a person to know? He could have been thinking about fishing tackle or whatever else his innocent self tended to ponder. Well, she would do nothing; he was married.

She got up and took his plate. As she turned away he took the wrist on her free arm and pulled her back. They smiled at each other and Audrey found a spot for their dishes. He kissed her and desire whooshed through her in an astounding way. She had forgotten. As she pressed against him her body turned soft and fluid, melded easily and naturally into his. The perfect fit was effortless and she wondered if it was because they had done it all before or if there were more magical reasons. The kiss lasted, they savoured one another's lips and tongues as they would choice fruits, ones that weren't available at the Safeway, fruits with names like candiola and yang tao. Audrey thought that it was possibly the kiss of her life.

Sex without booze wasn't something she had a lot of experience with. She had needed it, to provide the dimmer switch, the gauzy hue that allowed her the freedom to have fun with sex, to lose herself as best she could, or maybe find herself. Since she quit drinking she was sure the best of her life was behind her. The thought depressed her and she tried to make herself see that it didn't have to be so. The abandon of her tequila-drenched adventures was something that belonged to someone else. But there had to be other ecstasies. She didn't want to be like Lillian.

Suddenly the wooden stool made sense, with its rungs and its sturdiness. Audrey climbed up. "Frank, what about—"

"I had a vasectomy. And I don't have AIDS unless I got it over fifteen years ago and it still hasn't shown up."

"What about me? Aren't you worried about what I might give you?"

"No."

She laughed. And watched him look at her and felt his hands in her hair. They forced themselves to go slowly and the awkwardness of the stool helped prevent what might have been over too soon.

Laughter and whistles blew in from the lane and Frank reached over and turned out the lamp. They fell over onto the couch and lay quietly under the quilt.

"Too bad we don't smoke."

He laughed and kissed her temple. "Audrey, I never intended . . ."

She looked at him, wanting to hear him talk.

"I had no right . . . ," he began again.

"Yes, you did," she whispered. "Besides, no one's being unfaithful here. Let's not worry, okay Frank?"

"Okay." He sounded worried.

It occurred to Audrey that sex was wasted on the very young, and as she thought it, she had a vague remembrance of somebody older saying that very thing to her, years before. Then she remembered nights with certain people when it had been as right and good and deep as she had ever known it to be. When she was sixteen and twenty-four and thirty-eight, and now with Frank. She knew that she had felt joy at those times, not just the kind people see over their shoulders looking back, but a joy she'd had the sense or luck to feel profoundly at the time. Nothing good is ever wasted, thought Audrey; good things become part of the positive vibrations of the universe.

"Do you think you're going to live to be very old, Frank?" She snuggled in close.

"I don't know. Probably just a regular age, I guess. My parents were both kind of young when they died but I'm in better shape than they were."

"I think I'm going to live to be really old. There are so many things I haven't got the hang of yet, simple stuff, you know, that I should have figured out years ago. I'm going to need time to sort of wise up. I mean, until a couple of years ago I didn't realize that I walked around with toothpaste on my face half the time, attached to my lips, you know? Someone at work mentioned it to me and now I have a good look in the mirror after I brush my teeth and sure enough it's always there and I take care of it. I know that's not a big thing, but it's an obvious thing and I didn't get it."

Frank laughed. "Yeah, I remember that toothpaste thing. I never really thought much about it."

"Really? You remember me having toothpaste on my face? Why on earth didn't you mention it?"

"I don't know. I guess it didn't seem important."

Audrey sighed. "No, I guess it wasn't."

Frank turned onto his elbow and kissed Audrey's eyelids shut. He touched her face gently and licked her lips. She opened her eyes and watched him say, "I hope you live forever and get all your stuff figured out."

There was a timid knock at the porch door and the two of them froze there in the dark.

"Who is it?" Audrey was finally able to say.

There was a nervous clearing of a throat. "Your windshield wipers, ma'am. Sorry to bother you so late but I got held up at a couple of my other stops. I saw a light on in the house so I thought someone must be up."

"Just leave them there on the step or take them with you, and please take my phone number and address off your list and never bother me again. It was a big mistake."

"Shall I just show you—"

"No!"

He scurried off into the night.

Then it was just the wind in the trees till the first big drops of rain splatted onto the cement of Audrey's little patio.

Rain fell on that Saturday night. It fell on the Canadian prairies and on the western coastal regions of Mexico, all part of the same great system. It had been a dry season so far and the earth and water beds were in need. The rain came for several hours, and birds and other wildlife responded with happy water-receiving movements. Even some people, with their hairdos and alligator shoes, leaned into the wet and let it run over them.

Audrey and Frank stepped naked into the downpour; it was dark enough in the yard.

Iggy and Iris faced the sky and the water drenched them through.

Arthur had smelled the rain before it came and set up a sleeping place on his front veranda. It was an occasion and he wanted to give it its proper due, he wanted to think about it.

Spring rain fell into the cracks of so many winter souls.

Lillian hid from the rain as from an enemy.

Honey didn't notice.

Chapter Thirteen
South

They sat on the cedar deck on the ocean side of the house. The sun was just up and early risers were making the first footprints in the sand. Dog-walkers mainly, who encouraged, to varying degrees, the rambunctious joy of their charges who bounded hither and thither down the beach. It looked like a brand new day, but for Iris and Iggy the night wasn't over yet. Neither of them welcomed the morning light. It added a further strangeness to the circumstances. The darkness had acted as a cushion; it had made touching possible and provided a background for Iggy's confused murmurings of comfort. Words came less easily now and Iris was so subdued Iggy didn't know if he should go or stay.

"I don't usually go into the greenhouse, it's such a horrid place. I don't usually seek him out to say good night." Her eyes filled again with tears and Iggy moved closer. "Why'd I go there last night, Iggy? I don't want to have seen him. I don't want to carry that around with me for the rest of my life."

Iggy had walked home with Iris the night before and left her at the gate. She pointed to the light in the greenhouse and said it wasn't unusual for Ernest to work late into the night. Iggy was walking down the bumpy road that led back to his hotel when she ran stumbling up behind him, crazy-eyed and mute. He hurried back with her to the house and she was finally able to say, "I think Ernest is dead."

Iggy wished she knew for sure because he didn't want to have to look at him. The first thing he did was phone for an ambulance; he felt great satisfaction at making the call successfully. There had been times in Mexico when he had felt like ripping phones off walls when his efforts to use them proved fruitless.

He turned to Iris. "I guess we should see if there's anything we can do to help him." Iggy didn't want to blow air into a dead man's mouth, especially a dead man he hated, but he knew he had to try.

"No, Iggy. His head's blown off." Iris' eyes were huge and she started to shake uncontrollably. Iggy put his arms around her and led her to a couch where they sat, still wet with rain, holding onto each other until the ambulance arrived.

The men whose job it was to see to the business of violent death were packing up their things and getting ready to leave. The bag containing what had once been Ernest Kuntz had been removed an hour earlier.

"Cremation," Iris had said. "The sooner the better." She had phoned Ernest's lawyer and together they produced all of the dead man's wishes in his tiny meticulous handwriting.

A policeman and another man in a suit walked out onto the deck. "We'll be leaving now, Ms. Blowers. We'll be in touch."

Iris stood up. "Okay, Officer, thank you."

"Will you be all right?" the policeman asked.

"Yes, thanks, my friend Mr. Strand is here to help me."

Iggy stood up and tried to look like someone who had a history of handling difficult situations with extraordinary skill. He was going to have to be more careful with himself.

Paul Syms should have been the name he gave the cops. He'd have to tell Iris. When he saw the officials to the door he caught a glimpse of a solemn-looking Tomas heading towards the greenhouse with a wheelbarrow full of cleaning supplies.

Back on the deck he asked Iris the question that had been nagging at him. "Why do you think of the greenhouse as a horrid place?"

"Oh. You can go and have a look if you like."

"What am I going to find there?"

"His flowers, they weren't grown for their beauty, they were experiments. Some were for the restaurant and the house, but he grew other things. The cross-breeding that he did, in search of I don't know what, produced horrible ugly things, like nothing I'd seen or smelled before."

She shuddered. "They smelled awful. I never looked closely, I didn't want to have nightmares featuring his hideous growths. I tried not to go there but sometimes he made me. He nurtured 'his babies,' as he called them, then killed them. He wasn't a good man, Iggy."

Iggy was so cold he couldn't imagine ever being warm again, and he was also scared. He wanted to run from this place.

"You'd best try and get some sleep," he said. "Let's go inside. Is it okay if I make a fire?"

"There's no wood, I'm afraid. We don't use the fireplace much."

Iggy noticed the little dog from the night before at the bottom of the stairs. His two front paws were on the first step leading up to the deck and he smiled up at Iggy who ran down to greet him, so great was his surprise and pleasure at seeing a familiar face.

"Iris, look who's here!" He scratched the dog's ears and felt a little silly when Iris didn't respond.

"Honey didn't come home last night," she said instead.

"Oh? Is that unusual?" The dog's stiff fur was matted and plastered damply against its thin frame. "I'm going to call him Lewis. Come, Lewis. Come sit on the deck."

"Good heavens, Iggy. That creature is absolutely filthy, and he'll be covered with fleas."

"I'll give him a bath."

"Not in my bathtub you won't."

"Don't worry. I'll do it in the yard. I'll get Tomas to help me."

"Poor old Tomas. I think I ask too much of him. Please don't bother him with this, Iggy."

"Okay. Sorry. What's this about Honey? Sit, Lewis!" Lewis kept on standing but seemed to catch on to his name right away and wagged his shortened tail.

"Well, it's just, it's never happened before, her not coming home. She stays out late and gets up to all kinds of stuff but she's never not come home. It worries me because of what happened. What if she did come home and saw Ernest like that? Or what if he did it in front of her or—"

"Hey, wait. Don't go imagining all kinds of things that didn't happen. Heap picked her up, didn't he? She probably just spent the night at his place."

"Maybe. I guess so."

"Iris, why don't you try and rest for a while? If you like, I could look for Heap and Honey. I have his address." He found the matchbook in his pocket but it was soaked. "Oh, I guess I don't. Do you know where he lives?"

"No. That's stupid, isn't it? I know he lives a little further up the hill but I don't know where exactly. He's always so around I never really think of him actually living anywhere."

"It doesn't matter. Like you said, he's around. He'll turn up. They'll both show up before long."

"Yeah, you're probably right. But I feel worried. Odd as our relationship has been, there's a kind of kinship between Honey and me. I feel it anyway. She probably doesn't."

They went in the house, leaving Lewis to his own devices. Iggy drew Iris into the living room, where they sat down. "I guess it's the motherless thing," she said. "My mum was nuts, you know. I never got to know her very well."

"What? I didn't know that."

"Yeah."

There was a neatly folded blanket on one end of the couch that Iggy picked up and spread over their knees as they talked. Iris moved out from under her portion without touching it so Iggy wrapped it in tight around his legs.

"Is she still around?" he asked. "What about your dad?"

"He's still alive; my mum died quite a while ago. She never got better, ever in her life."

"When you say nuts, what do you mean exactly?" Iggy removed his sandals and put his feet up under him on the couch. His toes were like ice.

"Well, insane, wacko, crazy. It started out small but in the end she was labelled a full-fledged paranoid schizophrenic."

"Full-fledged, eh? Were you around when she got worse?"

Iris sank lower into the couch. "Maybe you've heard about the Allan Memorial Institute. Dr. Cameron? He got to be pretty big news after he was dead."

"Mm-hmm, yeah. I remember reading about it."

"My mum was one of his patients. He turned her into a zombie. I mean, I don't know how she would have made out otherwise, but, well, you read about it."

"Good Christ." Iggy rubbed his arms vigorously, trying to make up for the lack of heat in this semi-tropical country.

"Yeah. The man was dangerous but no one seemed to get it till after he was dead. Or, if they did, they didn't speak up. He was king of the psychiatrists in those days. And he wasn't breaking any laws. My dad was rich, is rich, so he sought the very best for my mum and came up with Dr. Ewan Cameron. What a joke!"

"Didn't I hear something about him and LSD?" Iggy stood and examined the cold fireplace. There weren't even any old ashes to push around.

"Yeah, you did. It was used as part of the drug therapy, so you can imagine."

Iris and Iggy had had some wacked-out times twenty-odd years back, ranging from euphoria in the dunes with the Beatles and the sunshine to endless dark nights in their dingy green and brown room where she clung to him in the clutches of a terror that he couldn't see and she wouldn't share. He thought he experienced glimpses of what she went through but he always pulled himself back. He hadn't given himself to it the way she had.

"My mum was fragile; it wiped her out and she never really made it back. She was afraid of me when she came home and that was way worse than being ignored, which was pretty much the way it was for most of my life. I knew I hadn't done anything to frighten her but I felt as though I had. I felt like a scary person."

Iggy's jaw was tight with the cold. He wanted a warm sleep before hearing any more.

Iris continued, "My dad encouraged me to leave since I upset her so much. I went to live with an aunt and uncle who lived close by. I didn't have to change schools or anything. It was okay. I stayed there through high school, visited my folks a bit, but it was never any good. Finally in '67 I figured, 'Fuck it. I don't have to be here.' That's when I came to Mexico. When I met you on the beach I'd been here a couple of years."

Iggy sat down beside Iris. The leather couch felt clammy and miserable through his clothes. "Why didn't you tell me then?"

"I don't know. I didn't really get what had happened to her at that point, I guess. It wasn't until 1977 that the whole story came out about that creepy doctor. And I guess I still felt guilty. I thought it was all my fault and I didn't want anyone to know . . . what kind of person I was." Tears sprung to her eyes. "It sounds pretty stupid, doesn't it?"

"Oh, Iris." Iggy held her and she felt so small, even smaller than the night before. She'd always had so little armour, been hurt so easily, even by her friends. Their jealousies and other thoughtless behaviour had made her feel she was doing something wrong, behaving badly; she'd felt blameworthy. Iggy had blamed her too, for keeping him out in those days. He wanted to protect her now, like before, but he knew her safety was ultimately out of his hands. And he was so tired.

She lay her head on his shoulder and let the tears stream down her face.

"Where's your father now?"

"As far as I know he's still there, in the house I grew up in. I don't keep in touch. I did till my mum died but then his letters dropped off and I didn't feel like trying anymore. He remarried soon after she died so he's not alone as far as I know."

"You're an only child, right?"

"Mm-hmm."

Iggy's clothes were dry in spots but where they were still damp, like around his collar, they touched him like icy fingers. He started to shiver.

"Do you still like your father?" His lips were blue and he had trouble forming the words clearly.

Iris looked at him. "Oh Iggy, you've got to get out of those clothes. You're freezing to death."

"He sounds like a primo asshole to me."

"Oh God, it's not worth it. I was mad for years, at him and at Dr. Cameron who had to go and die before I could kill him. But it's too hard being angry all the time."

"How could he have let it happen? How could he have kicked you out?" Iggy knew it was time to shut up.

"Maybe I will try to lie down for a while. . . . Iggy?"

"Yeah?"

"Could you please not go anywhere for a while? I've got lots of clothes you could change into. You could have a shower, a bath, eat, sleep, whatever. I just can't stand the thought of going to sleep and waking up and you not being here."

"I'll be here. For sure. Iris?"

"Yeah?"

"Since when is your last name Blowers?"

"Since forever."

"I thought it was Flowers."

She smiled. "I wish it was Flowers. Much prettier than Blowers, don't ya think?"

"Well, whaddya know? This is a revelation. Is your first name really Iris?"

"No."

"You're kidding. What is it?"

"Promise you won't laugh?"

"I promise."

"Bernice."

Iggy laughed.

"Thanks a lot! You said you wouldn't laugh. It's awful, isn't it?"

"You don't look anything like a Bernice Blowers. How can someone look so absolutely unlike their name?"

"Well, thanks. I don't want to look like a Bernice Blowers."

"Well, you don't."

"See ya later Iggy."

"You bet."

It was easy to work out because there was hot and cold running water outside the house. Tomas brought a wash-tub and soap and even some flea powder and the promise of a collar later in the day when he went for supplies.

Iggy invited Lewis into the backyard and under the warmth of the morning sun gave him a bath. He rinsed and soaped and scrubbed and rinsed till the tubs of water were clear and the little dog squeaked with cleanliness. His feet were cut in spots, with sharp pebbles embedded between the pads. Iggy worked patiently with his paws, soaking and cleaning and fashioning a pair of antiseptic socks. The dog loved the ministrations and sat still while Iggy took sticks of cotton dipped in alcohol and gently probed his ears, and bathed his eyes with warm water that washed away the sleep of his whole life.

Which wasn't that long a life, it turned out. He was very thin, but after his bath he had the look of a much younger dog. Iggy fluffed him up with a towel and his fur was blond and curly. Lewis waited there in the sun while Iggy went for two dishes. One he filled with water, the other with broken-up bits of hamburger he found in Iris' fridge. The dog ate tentatively, furtively, but he ate it all.

Iggy found a blanket and laid it down, part in sun and part in shade so the dog could make up his own mind. He picked sun for now and lay down and slept.

Chapter Fourteen

Honey awoke and left Heap's bed. She had never been to his little house before. She took her coffee to the small front room that overlooked the houses down the hill. The sky was so pale it was almost white in the early morning light. Honey's thoughts weren't on what lay before her so it took a few minutes for her to realize that Heap's house looked directly down into Iris and Ernest's backyard. It was a long way down but from where she stood Honey could make out the coffee table on the patio.

He put his hands on her shoulders and she swung around and looked into his worried face.

"I don't want to lose you," he said.

"Do you spy on me, Heap?" Honey was cautious, searching slowly, to find out exactly what this meant.

"I do, yes. Please don't hate me."

"You spy on me and you still say you love me." Her voice was barely a whisper, her face white and still as the sky.

"Yes. Please know that. I love you. I hated him. But I love you. I haven't known what to do."

Honey saw the high-powered binoculars sitting on the window sill. She sat down and thought about yesterday on the patio and other days in other rooms with blinds up and lights on, the way he liked it. She looked up at Heap and could think of nothing to say. This man had been her only hope and she couldn't believe that he loved her. How could he love her?

They watched Tomas and his wheelbarrow make their slow progress across the lawn to Ernest's greenhouse.

"Honey, can you still care for me when you know I've been watching you like this?"

"Heap, I don't see how it matters what you've been doing. All I can think of is what you've seen me doing."

"I didn't plan to watch you. It just happened once when you came into my line of vision, and after what I saw . . . I couldn't not watch. It was just a fluke that you turned out to be you. I didn't realize it at first when we met but then, when you told me you lived with old Iris . . . Honey, I want to help. I've already started."

"How? How can you help me?"

Heap sat down on the couch beside her. "I killed him. I killed Ernest last night."

Chapter Fifteen
North

Audrey awoke to find Craig staring at her. It would have been scary if she hadn't known him. She spoke to her cat and he nestled in beside her.

Frank.

And Lillian.

She forced herself out of bed. The alarmed look on Craig's face as he stood on the landing forewarned her of what was at the bottom of the cellar stairs. There had been water in the basement. It had come in and gone out again while she slept. It wasn't a disaster, there was nothing of value down there. But there was an awful lot of stuff, much of it brought over from her dad's house.

Several years ago she'd had a huge garage sale at his place. She'd even found items in the basement pantry left over from the grandmother days, canned and bottled things that she threw out without looking too closely. She sold her banjo, her Beatles memorabilia and her lava lamp. Everything else was easily forgotten but she immediately regretted the sale of those items. She missed them even as she watched them being loaded into the backs of various station wagons. What didn't sell that day ended up in Audrey's basement. Now would be her chance to go through it once and for all and be ruthless about throwing things away.

The light on her answering machine was quiet. She took coffee out to the porch where yesterday's *Free Press* sat untouched. First things first.

The porch was screened in on three sides with shutters all around. Just a sturdily built lean-to really, but it was the reason she'd bought the place ten years ago. It, and the dancing shadows of plum trees on the old-fashioned wallpaper in the bedroom. She had viewed the house on a warm June evening when, happily for everyone involved, the house showed itself in its finest light. Those moving shadows stayed with her. They were the bits of magic she needed to help her with her decision. She gave the rest of the house a perfunctory once-over as she imagined herself lounging endlessly in the fresh air of the porch and dreaming in and out of the shadows on the bedroom wall.

A moving van rumbled down the back lane as Audrey settled on the couch. She wondered if the people who were moving had water in their basement. She was glad she wasn't them.

The porch wasn't fixed up for winter but Audrey used it long into the fall and in the early spring before the snow was gone. Many a dark chilly morning found her bundled in winter wear and covered with quilts, sipping coffee from her Thermos cup and reading by the light of her garage-sale lamp.

She had painted the walls white as soon as she moved in. That was the only real decorating she'd done, other than putting down a small rug on the floor of Spanish tiles (a marvellous extravagant whim on the part of the previous owner) and filling the place with greenery in the summer months.

The red stool had sat behind the cash register in her grandfather's general store. Audrey had asked for it at the auction, a million years ago. It reminded her of the long summers of her youth, too precious by far to be lumped in with the coolers and counters and such.

The only drawback to the porch was that when the shutters on the north side were open there was a chance she would be forced into an encounter with her neighbour, Dicky Putz. He had killed Craig's predecessor. Putz drove his car like a small-town hood and the rye and Cokes that he drank continually only fed the aggression. The small cat had been killed instantly but Putz wasn't sorry and Audrey wanted nothing more to do with him. His voice was a high-pitched bark and it jarred her insides to hear him talk.

He was so unlike the quiet, gentle Arthur with his push mower and one-speed bicycle with carrier for groceries and library books. Manoeuvring the bike was no mean feat with that huge shoe, but he managed it when the ground was dry and took a bus when it wasn't. He knew he made a comical sight, he had said as much to Audrey; he heard the taunts of the children who hadn't been taught any manners.

Arthur feared Dicky Putz, so Audrey was glad she was in the middle as a buffer. He had said that guys like Putz with their loud sounds and violent vibrations made him feel hunted on bad days and filled him with a fear of that feeling on easier ones. When Putz trimmed hedges with a huge motorized insect of a tool or choreographed the construction of his new sidewalk, Arthur couldn't concentrate as long as the machines were turned on. It wasn't a fear of machinery. It was the man that filled him with unease.

He had confided to Audrey that his fear embarrassed him. And he felt he should be better at controlling the rage that coursed through him when he heard his neighbour barking greetings to passers-by. He used to feel that if he examined the Putz-noises to make sure they didn't involve him he would be able to get on with his day, but that didn't work. No matter how unconnected the disturbances seemed, they caused him trouble; like when the cement truck ripped the cable line away from his house during the World Series.

So he was glad he had Audrey there as protection and she felt good about providing it, though she didn't see it as amounting to much. She didn't fear Putz the way Arthur did, but she thought she understood the fear. It reminded her of something. She pointed out to Arthur that he might as well get used to it. Putz was the kind of guy who didn't move; his parents had lived and died in that house and he'd be there until the hydro man discovered his bloated body in the bathtub or some such.

Sunday morning was quiet, and Audrey sat looking out at the drenched spring world. The only sound was the water, barely dripping still from the new leaves and leaky eaves. The sun was barely up but felt warm already; spring would turn to summer today. She felt a moment of pure happiness and for a while she didn't move. Inklings of freedom and modest adventures effervesced beneath her surface.

By the time Frank drove up Audrey had showered and dressed in her oldest overalls and was getting ready to tackle the basement. They smiled at each other as he walked up the sidewalk towards her. She felt his smile in her solar plexus, where it fanned out and reached all her nether regions.

"Frank, hi, it's so early. I'm happy to see you. Do you want some coffee?"

"No thanks, I can't stay. I just wanted to say hi."

"Hi."

"Hi. How are ya?" He reached for one of her hands and held it in both of his.

"I'm fine. How are you?" She added her other hand to the pile.

"Fine too, I guess." They stood self-consciously attached for a moment or two and then let their hands fall free. Audrey's went to the pockets of her overalls and Frank's landed first on his hips and then up to the top of his head where they interlocked for a short stay.

"Any word on Lillian?" Audrey asked.

"No, I'm afraid not. Nothing here either, eh?"

"No. But in the light of day I don't feel as worried as I did last night. She's probably just hanging out in her wayward manner. The only difference really is that someone she doesn't know is dead. It probably looks too troublesome from where she stands. Do you know who the dead guy is yet?"

"No. I'll keep you posted though. We've been counting on the Iggy character to turn up but he's gone too, disappeared. I wonder if Lillian knows where he is." Frank began cracking his knuckles and Audrey wished he'd left them on top of his head.

"I don't think so," she said. "She sure seemed genuine to me, in not knowing what was going on."

"Yeah?"

"Yeah. I see you still do that thing with your knuckles."

"What? Oh. God, I'm sorry. Yeah, I guess I do. It drives everyone crazy. I don't know why I can't let it go. Sorry."

"Oh gosh, don't worry, Frank. I don't know why I mentioned it. Please forget I did."

"No, I know it's really annoying. My whole family yells at me for it."

"Are you sure you won't have some coffee? There's some made already."

"No. Thanks. I have to pick up Uncle Bosco at the airport right now and after that I'll likely be putting in a full day's work."

"Wow, talk about getting here pronto. That's great, Frank. Are the kids excited about him coming?"

"Well, no. Em's worried about her mum and doesn't figure she needs looking after, Garth lives inside the television, and Sadie admits she needs looking after but doesn't remember Bosco. So it's not all that exciting, I guess."

"Are you okay, Frank?"

"Yeah. Thanks for listening to me last night. Denise would slice me open if she knew I told anyone. She's not keen on this getting around."

Frank had told Audrey about the gap in Saturday afternoon, when he had been placing his wife in the detox centre. Again.

"I'm not going to tell people," Audrey said.

"I know you won't," Frank sighed. "I'm sorry. I shouldn't have said anything."

"It's okay. Don't worry, Frank. I'm sorry I mentioned your knuckles." She put her arm around his waist. "Everything'll be okay. It will."

"Thanks. Sorry. I better get going. . . . Um, Audrey?"

"Yes?"

"What did you mean last night when you said that bit about nobody being unfaithful to anyone?"

"Oh. Well, let's see." She withdrew her arm and plunged her hands into her pockets. "I hope I can explain what I thought I meant. Um, we're sort of connected, you and me, from a long time ago and last night was part of that, kind of an extension, a continuation of sorts. It wasn't something new, meant to interfere with you and Denise. It was you and me, old business. I guess it sounds a little hippy-dippy but I think it holds water."

"It sounds good to me. Audrey, I . . ."

"Oh, there's Arthur. Have you ever met him?"

"No, I haven't. I've seen him around on his bike but I've never really met him."

"Here, let's introduce you. He's a really neat guy."

Arthur was getting an early start on his yard work and was busy gathering his tools together.

"Morning, Arthur," Audrey called over the fence.

He looked up from his wheelbarrow and smiled. "Good morning, Audrey. And isn't it a beauty?"

"It sure is. That rain was grand, wasn't it?"

"It was so!" Arthur left what he was doing and made his way to the Audrey side of the yard. Even with his huge shoe he walked with an awkward limp.

"Did you get water in your basement?" she asked.

"No. At least, I haven't checked. Did you?"

"Yes, unfortunately."

"Oh, you poor dear."

"Did you?" asked Frank.

"Yeah."

Audrey pulled him towards the fence. "This is Frank Foote, the policeman I was telling you about. Frank, this is my good neighbour, Arthur Pointe."

The men shook hands over the low fence. Arthur offered to go and get the letter that Frank hadn't picked up but Audrey told him just to throw it away.

"I hope that means everything's all right," said Arthur shyly, not wanting to pry.

"Well, pretty all right, I guess, except for Lillian having disappeared."

"Oh, that poor soul."

Arthur had listened to Audrey call Lillian a disaster waiting to happen but he couldn't see how it applied to that sad weakened creature. Disaster seemed too strong a word for what someone of Lillian's energy level could make happen. He thought of her as one of the lost souls of the universe, whose biggest adventure would be her death, and death wasn't really a disaster. It might be Lillian's saviour and it could so easily claim someone so very low.

There had been times when Lillian had dropped by when her sister wasn't home. She had sat at Arthur's then, and watched him garden. They drank coffee or iced tea and shot the breeze a bit. She seemed to find him easy company, perhaps because he didn't expect anything from her and didn't find it necessary to talk all the time.

He supposed he saw her differently from the way Audrey did. To Audrey she seemed like a responsibility of sorts because they were related, but Arthur thought if Audrey could see Lillian without those messy blood ties, see her as separate, they could get on better. He tried once to make a suggestion to that effect but Audrey didn't get it. He would try again.

Arthur sometimes thought that losing a family at an early age could be nothing but good news for the orphan involved. It freed him up to see things clearly. There was inevitable fussing and fighting among the adults close to the dead parents but the orphan was free. Arthur felt extremely lucky. He was fond of Uncle Len and Aunt Joan but he didn't belong to them and they had let him go as soon as he was ready. He saw them, but not often and not in any parent-son kind of way. When he had told them how lucky he felt they had seemed to understand.

"Well, we'll leave you to it then, Arthur. See ya later."

"Okay, Audrey. Good to meet you, Frank."

"Same here, Arthur. See you again. Don't forget to check on that basement."

"Righto."

Arthur was pleased with Audrey's friend. He didn't want her to be lonesome and it seemed like ages since she'd had any kind of carryings-on with a man. The thought of Audrey's loneliness seemed far more poignant to him than his own. He wondered about that. Perhaps, then, her loneliness didn't amount to much from her point of view, as his didn't when he thought about it. Not likely. Logic didn't usually apply to feelings. And he heard so much about other people's loneliness.

Arthur seldom found his own aloneness to be troublesome. He had a way of enlarging his thoughts, or, rather, enlarging the expanse surrounding his thoughts to put them in a comfortable perspective, one that suited him; it was a meditation of sorts. The vastness of his reflections held him spellbound and he felt a great satisfaction in his daily life in spite of his considerable neuroses.

Alone, when the neighbourhood was quiet, he would take off his shoes for a spell. He would sit on the front veranda with his feet up, imagining himself walking through life with two long straight legs. He dreamed of tall women, shining ski slopes and sandy beaches where he was king. When he snapped out of it he felt rested, fresh, at ease. The pleasures he found in his reveries were very deep pleasures indeed.

But since Kenneth's discovery in the dumpster it had become more difficult for Arthur to relax. It was sweat and toil he needed now, hard work to help him past the nasty thoughts that were stuck like tar in his brain.

Chapter Sixteen

Dear Lily,

I hope I haven't caused you too much pain or trouble. It certainly wasn't part of my plan.

Life here seems out of my control and taking off looks to me like the only way. My fairly simple living is getting way too complicated with Chucky Junior flexing his muscle. He wants in, Lily, and I'm not up to it either way. It seems kind of unbelievable that this kind of stuff happens here but you've been around all this as long as I have so it probably doesn't surprise you. It's just as well, really, I'm too old for this shit. It sure wasn't the way I planned to spend my life.

I'm not telling you where I'm going because, let's face it, I'm a criminal. I've paid rent on the apartment for a full year so you aren't left in the lurch. I just hope you didn't take me seriously tonight when I threw my tantrum and kicked you out. I was just so wretched about leaving everything behind. Do what you like with my stuff, walk away from it if it suits you.

I wish you well, Lily, and I'm sorry for all I've done to hurt you.

In friendship,
Ignatius

Fred Sharples stared at the letter on his desk. He had found it on his way to work when, on a whim, he had stopped by the Strand place to have another poke around. It was a small bit of pay dirt that answered a few questions. It was probably a drug death but who the hell was the dead guy? Fred had a call in to Frank.

There was a knock at his door.

"Come in," Fred shouted.

The door opened and a small pale face peered in.

"Can I help you with something, Miss?" Fred was on his feet. The girl looked like she needed help just putting one foot in front of the other. For Fred it was love at first sight. He wanted to carry her home and take care of her. He helped her into a chair and repeated his question.

"My name is Frances Hicks and I'm here to identify Henry Gladue." She sounded stronger than she looked. Her voice was deep and rich and steady and Fred started to sweat.

She sounded like the girl in his dream, the one who talked to him when he couldn't hold back his tears. She reassured him and brushed the hair away from his eyes, long hair like in university days. He had never known anyone like the girl in the dream, anyone as soft and full of love. He had seen girls that he thought might be like her but they always disappointed him.

For a moment he didn't know what she was talking about, then realized that she was here to claim their mysterious corpse. They did what was necessary. Frances trembled and cried and Fred looked after her. He held her and soothed her and stayed with her.

He wanted to keep her, so he took her back to headquarters to question her about the relationship between

Henry Gladue and Ignatius Strand, and about anything else he could think of.

"I know Henry knew Iggy," she said, "but not well. We used to buy dope from him. We've both been clean awhile now." She took a sip of the coffee Fred had made for her. "Where did he live?"

"Out on the south highway in a three-storey walk-up."

That road was sprinkled with motels, fast-food outlets, automotive-type shops and square three-storey apartment buildings circa 1950. Further south, buildings grew scarce, just the odd gas station and market gardener's home. And then open prairie stretching out till it hit the sky, split down the middle by the old two-lane highway. It was the road Frances came in on and the one Henry had followed into the city the day before.

"He came in to look for a truck part. He forgot his wallet, probably checked into Iggy's place to see if he could borrow a few bucks. I know he wasn't there to buy dope. For one thing, he didn't have any cash."

Frances' eyes filled with tears again when the folly causing Henry's death became clear to her. It was a mistake. How could there be such a mistake?

Fred put his arm around her.

"We were gonna get married," she said uselessly.

Fred's phone rang. It was Frank calling from the airport. Fred filled him in as best he could with Frances sitting there. He was very careful to use words that wouldn't hurt her. He spoke of Henry Gladue with gentle genuine respect.

Chapter Seventeen
South

The midday heat drove Iggy outside to a shady spot under an old avocado tree. Lewis noted his arrival and adjusted himself so his chin rested on one of Iggy's feet. Then he went back to sleep. Iggy had a book that he'd found in Ernest's study, a medical book about mutilation techniques practised by various peoples of the world. He looked at the pictures of the women with their facial scars and tattooed lips and was relieved to read that many of those old ways were no longer practised. Certain rites continued, however, and only in the last couple of decades were they being questioned and very gradually abandoned.

"I see you found yourself some reading material." Iris startled him. He hadn't heard her approach over the soft green grass.

He closed the book suddenly, embarrassed by his fascination with the grotesqueries before him on his lap. Then he felt like a fool, like the small boy he had once been, caught by the tall rectangular mother. She had teased him mercilessly, anytime, anyplace, in front of her canasta ladies, or anyone who would listen. They looked at her askance; he knew even then that it was his mother they wondered about, not him, but that was just as bad.

"Hi, Iris, did you sleep?"

"I did, for a little while. What's with Lewis' feet?"

"Oh. They were a bit cut up so I made him some make-shift socks with antiseptic ointment on the inside. Tomas helped me."

Iris gave him a sidewise look.

"Sorry. But he wanted to help. He's even gonna pick up a flea collar when he's out for supplies. And I defleaed Lewis already, so you can touch him if you want." He gave the dog's ears a scratch. "Doesn't he look great?"

Lewis sat up smartly for Iris' inspection but she just sat down at Iggy's other foot and rested her head and arms on her knees, which were covered by a long skirt printed with moons and stars. Her hair was shower wet and smelled like lemons.

"Are you okay?" she asked.

"Yeah, I'm okay. Are you okay?" Iggy wanted to fuck Iris but knew how inappropriate that was. He knew if it was to happen it would be a long convoluted trail and he didn't know if he was up to it. But he was proud of his ability and he wanted to show it to her. He wanted to make her come with his dick, he wanted to fuck her into coming. He hadn't known how twenty-odd years ago so it would be a pleasant surprise for her, like for Lily. But he couldn't very well boast about it beforehand.

"Yeah, I guess so," she replied. "I don't feel much of anything, really. I mean, I've dreamed of this day, I've longed for it, but now it's here I don't know what to do with it. So far, anyway."

"Maybe it's the awful way it happened," ventured Iggy. "It's kind of hard to feel happy about something so violent even if the end result is something you wanted."

After some circling, Lewis lay back down, this time with his eyes open. Iggy tousled the curly blond head and the little dog made appreciative sounds in his throat.

"Ernest wouldn't have killed himself. He despised people who took the easy way out. Not that that's any kind of proof, but knowing him like I did, it just seems so . . . unlikely somehow."

"Whoa-oa back, Iris? The cops didn't even hint at foul play."

"No. They didn't, did they? That's a good thing, I think. I mean, who needs all the razzamatazz that would go along with that? This way it'll all be over soon and everyone who knew him can start forgetting about him."

"Who would have . . . ?"

Iris stood up abruptly. Her blue eyes were the exact colour of the wide expanse of sky behind her. They looked like part of that sky, as if the rest of her face were just a cutout placed over the blue to give the impression that something human stood there. "I wish it had been me," she said.

Iggy sat for a moment, feeling nervous and a bit frightened. The space between them was too big and he didn't want it getting any bigger. It allowed for too many odd thoughts. He didn't want to lose track of who Iris was. He left Lewis under the tree and followed her into the house.

"I just hope they're long gone, far away from here." She was loading the dishwasher with mugs left over from the policemen and their tea.

"Who?" Iggy sat down. There was a little dish of shells and oddly shaped rocks on the table. He picked out two to examine more closely.

"I don't know, whoever killed Ernest. Heap and Honey? I don't know. I'm so confused, I feel like I'm in a dream."

"Wow, this is a fossil." Iggy looked up from the rock he held gently in the palm of his hand. "You think Heap and Honey killed Ernest?"

"I don't know. But they seem to have disappeared and that's a puzzle, isn't it?" She sounded as though she were talking to a small child.

"I don't know. I don't feel like I know anything about what's going on and I don't think I'm any help so I think I'll be running along." Iggy was hurt by her tone. And he had his own things to worry about, like being rich and free.

"Yes, all right."

Iggy returned the fossil to its dish and walked into Ernest's study to put the book back where he'd found it. He was struck again by the narrow scope of the material on the shelves. There weren't a lot of books for an educated man and those there were dealt with only two subjects: gardening and African medicine. He couldn't resist commenting, "Ernest has a pretty esoteric book collection."

"Yeah, his interests weren't all that broad." Iris was smoking a cigarette at the kitchen table.

"Well, I guess I'll be going then."

"Yes. Well, thanks for everything. You were a big help to me."

He kissed her on the forehead and left on the beach side, completely forgetting about Lewis under the backyard tree.

Iggy was disgusted with himself. He felt like a selfish, inept asshole who didn't know how to help and offer comfort. He shouldn't have had to leave. Big Heap Huggins would have known what to do for her. He knew how to be a friend. Tears poured down Iggy's face as he walked into the wind, fists clenched at his sides. His exhaustion overwhelmed him but he couldn't imagine ever sleeping again. Perhaps he would die of tiredness; it would serve him right.

When he was a ways down the beach he turned to look at the house that Iris had shared with Ernest. She stood on the deck staring after him. He felt her dark blue eyes pleading with him to come back. Only he didn't know if he was making it up or not. He knew she was standing there staring but maybe her eyes weren't even focussed on him, she could have been watching a seagull or some inner thought. No. He felt her pull. She reached for him, he knew she did. He stood for a while, neutral in the sand, then made his way slowly back.

Chapter Eighteen
North

Fred wheeled his Ford into the yard of the home that Frances had shared with Henry Gladue. When Frances looked up she was stunned by what she saw. The house looked like nobody lived in it. There was no paint on the rotting boards and the whole structure leaned to one side. Upstairs windows were broken, with pieces of cardboard over some of them to keep out the wind and rain. They would have to be replaced now, after last night's storm. The front steps were gone. She had never thought about that before. They just never went in that way. There was nothing moving in the yard, no tree, no dog, no blade of grass. It was a dead patch.

Frances had never seemed right to herself in her whole life except when she was with Henry. She had known the night before that he was dead. The anchorwoman on the local television station broke the news. She didn't mention a name, she didn't know it yet, but Frances did. The anchorwoman hadn't used the phony death voice that most of them put on for stories like that and Frances had been grateful.

She looked at Fred and couldn't imagine what he must be thinking.

"Would you like to come in for a cup of coffee?"

"Yes. Frances, is there anywhere else you can go? Family or a friend?"

She slammed the car door as he spoke so she didn't have to answer. She didn't want him feeling sorry for her.

They walked toward the house. It sat in a sea of black mud. Fred wouldn't be able to save his shoes. Nothing held the ground so it blew away in dry weather and turned to muck in wet. Henry's broken truck sat knee-deep in the gumbo. Soggy cardboard pieces lay in the mud below the bedroom window. Frances remembered waking up that morning and recalling that Henry was dead. She had lain there, freezing. The rain had come in and soaked the covers on one end of their bed. And Henry hadn't come home because he was dead.

She started to cry now. Fred smoothed her hair and gave her his clean white handkerchief. It smelled like cloves and brought back a memory of a taste or a smell from a long-ago Christmas. She hoped he wouldn't leave her there alone.

Chapter Nineteen

Summer had run itself into town and Audrey hoped it wasn't here to stay. Spring was better, when all the bounty lay ahead. She was afraid summer would go by too quickly, and would have preferred it never to begin at all. The warm season was short on the Canadian prairies and there was pressure to get out there and enjoy it. She thought about that as she flipped the pages of an old photo album, rescued from the soggy basement. The pressure didn't feel as compelling as it had in former years. She stood and stretched, breathing deeply. She was pleased with herself.

"Audrey!" It was Frank again at the screen door.

He accepted her offer of lemonade and they took the photos outside to the porch.

Audrey laughed, "Look at this one of you, Frank. You look like you can't decide whether to fold your arms or leave them dangling at your sides."

"Yeah, I look like a simp. Look at this one of you. You look like your head is fitted on backwards."

"I do not."

"You do so. Look at this one of you and Lily smiling right at each other. That's a beautiful picture. Who took that?"

"I don't know. I don't remember that at all." Audrey

removed it from the book to have a closer look. "It is a nice picture, isn't it?"

"Yeah."

"Maybe I'll stick it to my fridge." She closed the book. "No new developments?"

"Nothing on Lillian. We've stopped looking for her as someone connected to the murder. It's up to you if you want to keep a search going."

"Hmm. I'll have to think about that. It probably doesn't make much sense to keep on looking for her. I mean, why really?" Audrey smoothed her fingers over the photograph. There they were, smiling happily and truly at each other. There was nothing hooded or sideways about it.

"Yeah, well, it's up to you. Fred found a letter to Lily from Iggy."

"Really?"

Frank described the note Fred had shown him when he dropped by the station. And he told her about Chucky Junior and Henry Gladue and Henry's girlfriend, Frances.

"Oh my God," Audrey said. "These people, Henry and Frances. This is really horrible, Frank."

"Yeah."

"Talk about being in the wrong place at the wrong time."

"Yeah." Frank drained his glass.

"Will Lily get to have a look at the letter? I mean, it is hers. And it means a place to stay and all."

"Yeah. After we're done with it I'll give it to you, so if she turns up . . ."

"Oh boy, I hope she does now. She should know this stuff."

Audrey went into the house for more lemonade. She filled Frank's glass and they sat side by side and quiet.

She picked up the photograph of herself and her sister and held it beside her face. "Do I still look like that person in the picture?"

Frank laughed. "Yes, you do."

"Yeah, sure."

"You look wonderful, Audrey. You look way better than the person in the picture." He touched her lips with his fingertips and kissed her on the very edge of her mouth.

Flushing, she reopened the book of photographs and flipped through the pages. "Thanks," she said.

"We're picking up Chucky Purse and his brother Kirby," Frank said. "We don't have anything concrete but Lillian's letter's a start."

"Is that really their names? Chucky and Kirby Purse?"

" 'Fraid so." Frank chuckled.

"Yuck. I hope it was them."

"Yeah. It looks more and more as if Henry Gladue was just unlucky. According to Frances Hicks he and Iggy were about the same size. And they both had short darkish hair, at least that's how she remembers Strand. She hasn't seen him in over a year. So it's easy to see how someone who didn't know either of them well could have made the mistake. It's a basement apartment with a northern exposure, real dingy and dark. A killer in a hurry would have leapt for joy at the sight of his quarry sitting like a duck under headphones."

"Frances Hicks. That poor woman. What was she like?"

"Small. Quiet. Sad. Fred gave her a ride home. He seemed quite taken with her."

Audrey and Frank took the overgrown path that led down to the water's edge. They walked till they came to a small clearing at a bend in the river. They sat in the dappled sunlight filtered through the huge old cottonwoods.

She told him about a time when they were young when Lillian had set up an animal hospital in the backyard. It started with a mourning dove that had hit the dining-room window. She sat with it at a distance, not wanting to frighten it. The poor bird must have broken its neck or some other important part because it died there in the garden. But not alone. Lily slowly crept closer and petted the silken head as it gave up its struggle.

And she had an earthworm named Floyd that she taped together with iodine and band-aids after it had been sliced in half by the boy next door. It died too. Actually it was already dead. But she devoted her days to these casualties of the animal kingdom, named them all, and invited neighbourhood dogs and cats to be her assistants.

There was a quiet splash from further along the bank.

"Let's have a look," said Audrey, standing.

They rounded the bend in time to see something disappear beneath the water close to shore. When it resurfaced they saw that it was a huge old turtle and it wasn't alone. There were two, and they frolicked comically, heavily. They chased and surprised each other, and best of all, they pressed their thick wet necks together as they stretched from their shells to the warming rays of the sun. Frank and Audrey exchanged an excited glance and watched, amazed and joyful, the rare sight. The turtles were so at home, so comfortable in the shallow mucky water. They were born there and they would die there, simple ancient extentions of the natural riverbed, so close to the filthy traffic on the bridge. Audrey would remember those turtles and haul them out of her memory from time to time to cheer herself up.

Arthur and Kenneth watched them come up from the river. They sat in Arthur's upstairs veranda with its wide southern exposure. Arthur was on the couch with his feet up, relaxed in the presence of his old friend. Kenneth's big bulk was settled into an easy chair where he sat thoughtfully, drinking from a long bottle of Alberta beer. On the table between them sat one of Arthur's shoes on a piece of newspaper. It was huge and grotesque, made more so by the stench of garbage that clung to it. There were shiny patches where unknown fluids stuck and didn't dry up. Arthur hadn't wanted to touch it after Kenneth dropped it off on Friday, but he hadn't wanted to throw it away either. He studied it from a distance till he thought he understood what it had been used for. His friend had been in a hurry on Friday and hadn't been able to stay for a visit. They talked now about the shoe and other things.

"Audrey seems to have a new friend," Arthur observed.

"Great choice. That guy's a cop. He's also married."

"Oh dear. I knew he was a policeman but I didn't realize he was married. I wonder if Audrey knows."

"I'm sure she does. They go way back, those two. High-school days. He's a nice guy, Frank Foote. I like him. It's not his style to fuck around on the wife. Maybe this is just some kind of unusual platonic thing."

"I don't think so." Arthur had heard them on the porch the night before.

He looked back at the filthy object on the coffee table. "Did I ever tell you about the two hoodlums who ran off with my shoe last fall?"

"No."

"It was horrible."

"What happened?" Kenneth took a long swallow of beer.

"I was at the library and when I came out it was snowing so it was slippery on the way home. I fell off my bike. Two young fellows accosted me and ran off with my big shoe. I couldn't ride my bike without it so I came home on foot for another pair and went back for the bike. At least it was still there."

"Nasty little buggers."

"Yes, I worry about life in this last part of the twentieth century, Kenneth, the way it seems to be blindly hurtling along. I think that must be why parents are neglecting to teach their children manners. Caught up in the hurtling, they think they don't have time."

Kenneth sighed, "I guess."

"Those kids who took my shoe were probably thirteen. What on earth are they going to be up to by the time they're nineteen?"

"Do you think it was the youths? Who would have used your shoe in this way, Arthur?"

"No, it wasn't the youths. This isn't that shoe."

"Who then?"

"Nate." Arthur started trembling.

"Nate who? Who's Nate?"

"Nate Underhill, just a man I know, knew. I haven't seen him in ages." He covered up with his afghan and tucked it in around himself.

"Are you sure it was him?"

"Of course I'm sure. For goodness' sake, Kenneth, I think I know who has what pair of shoes."

"Are you okay, Arthur?"

"Yes, thanks, just a little chilly."

Arthur had a great fear of being without his shoes. He had dreams about shoemakers. In the bad ones he was unable to find one willing to build up his shoes, or he couldn't find one at all. His local shop would be boarded up and when he searched for a new one, evil cobblers would laugh at him or brush him off.

In the good dreams he simply visited his own shoemaker, Reg Childers, who'd been doing his shoes since taking over his father's shop years ago. The senior Reg had performed the service until his death. Arthur had been worried at first, in case Reg Jr. didn't measure up, but soon he came to appreciate the work of the younger man, who was actually about Arthur's age. He woke up from the good dreams feeling satisfied with work well done and with the overall state of his shoe collection.

"How many pairs do you have now?" Kenneth asked.

"I have nineteen at present, five of them kept outside the house in case it burns down or falls victim to some other disaster. There's one in the shed, one in the garage, one at your place, one next door with Audrey and one in a safety deposit box. There was a twentieth pair but this one no longer counts." He nodded at the mess on the table.

"Even if it wasn't Nate who actually did it, the shoes were his responsibility," Arthur continued. "I never did feel settled about that particular pair. I didn't know him very well, and as it turns out my uneasiness was for good reason. I should have known better than to leave my shoes with a slippery scoundrel. But he offered and I didn't want to refuse what I took to be a simple kindness."

"Have you spoken to him about it?"

"No."

"Why not?"

"I haven't felt up to it."

"Do you want to phone the police?"

"Of course not."

"How be we just mention it to Frank? We could do it casual like, out in the yard if they ever come out of the house again."

"Don't be ridiculous. I said I didn't want to go to the police," Arthur snapped.

"Okay, okay."

"I'm sorry, Kenneth. It's just, well, it's my shoes. I don't want people I don't know talking about them and asking me a whole lot of questions. They might make light of it and I don't think I could stand that. You and Audrey are really the only ones that know how many pairs I have and that I keep some of them in other places. And Nate. God, what a mistake that was."

"Who the hell is this guy? I've never even heard of him before."

"Oh, it was stupid. I met him on a train coming back from Vancouver, a long time ago. You know how train conversations go. You figure you're never going to see the person again so you end up giving him your life story, including the weird stuff, especially the weird stuff."

"Yeah, I know what you mean. It's a good chance to unload."

"Yes. Anyhow, he was a good listener and seemed kind enough. He offered to house a pair of my shoes and I took him up on it. I didn't see how it could hurt. In those days I was a little more frivolous. I would never do such a thing now!" Arthur pounded his fist on the table and jostled his shoe around some.

Kenneth was able to snatch his beer up in time. "No, you wouldn't. Look, maybe it's not such a terribly bad thing. I mean in the grand scheme of things, surely it isn't all that serious."

"Yes it is."

"Yeah, okay."

"He meant well, I'm sure of it. It was just that it was so long ago, the importance of it probably faded in his mind. I was so sure at the time that he got how important it was to me. I should have kept in touch but I didn't really want another friend I guess. I just checked in with him by phone about once a year to make sure he was still around and left it at that. He disappointed me terribly."

"I know he did, Arthur. I'm really sorry."

Kenneth finished his beer and got up to leave. "So, we had our seventh murder of the year yesterday morning. Did you see the paper?"

"No. Who? Where?"

"I don't know who. They're having trouble identifying the guy. It's not who they figured it was at first, so they're currently stumped."

"What do you mean, it's not who they figured it was at first? Who did they figure it was?"

"The guy who lived where the guy was found. But it turns out that guy has just disappeared. So they don't know who the hell it is or who did it or anything.

"Well, I'm off, old buddy." Kenneth picked up his empty and looked again at the shoe. "Try not to worry about this, Arthur. Do you want me to get rid of it for you? It's a bit of a mess, all that time spent in a dumpster."

"No. Thanks kindly, Kenneth. What do you mean the guy disappeared?"

"He's not around. The cops can't find him. Who knows, maybe he's the murderer. I don't know. Anyway, gotta go."

Arthur let Kenneth find his own way out. He sat looking out the window for a very long time. The twilight came and went before he made his way down the stairs to secure his home for the night.

"I don't think there's any need to keep looking for Lillian, officially I mean," said Audrey. They were in her bedroom and had, self-consciously at first, shed all their clothes.

"Okay. I'll phone somebody."

He kneaded the swollen muscles running down the middle of her back. She turned to him and smoothed his furrowed forehead with her fingers, massaging till the tension left his brow. He kissed her lips as he got up to fill the tub with water as hot as they could stand it. She took the soap from him and worked up a lather on his back and shoulders. She rested her face against his clean skin and he felt her heart beating against his back. He washed her feet with care not to tear the blisters left over from her week's work. Her tears fell down his back, she was so grateful for his tenderness. He made peppermint tea and brought it to her in bed. She listened to him as he talked about his daughter Em, the lonely one. He showed her what to do with her pillow to make her back more comfortable in the night. She promised to wake him in two hours so he could go to the hospital and visit his wife. He noticed the dancing shadows on her wall. She told him a boring story in a lazy voice designed to make him sleep.

Chapter Twenty
South

"Thanks for coming back," she whispered as he kissed her temple, the wisps of blonde and grey.

They lay on Iris' bed with all their clothes on.

"I love you Iggy, but I can't have sex with you. I can't have sex with anyone."

"That's okay, Iris. I understand." He lay back and took her hand.

"I don't feel sexual anymore, ever."

"How could that be, someone as beautiful as you?"

"It doesn't have anything to do with what I look like on the outside."

"Of course it doesn't. That was a really stupid thing for me to say." Iggy's hand was sweating and he wanted to let go but thought the action might be too abrupt and seemingly fraught with meaning.

"I miss it," Iris continued, "and I miss the way it used to feel to long to have sex with someone. I miss those feelings but I can barely recall them now. I can remember long nights of wakefulness, because of a need so big. Now I wish I had enjoyed that need more." She sighed, "It's like a death of sorts."

"Maybe it's not gone forever," said Iggy hopefully.

She smiled as she sat up on her elbow, releasing his hand.

"Is it because of Ernest?" he added.

She continued as though she hadn't heard him. "Different things keep me awake now."

"Like what?"

"Nothing. I'm being boring."

"No, you're not."

"Yes, I am. I'm even boring me with my troubles. I guess I should tell you about Ernest but I find him such a distasteful subject."

"You don't have to." Iggy clasped his hands across his chest as though prepared for burial.

"No. It'd be easier for you to understand some things if you knew him better, if you want to understand, that is."

"You know I do." At least I think I do, thought Iggy.

Iris lay back down. "The reason Ernest came to Mexico is that he lost his licence to practise medicine in Britain."

"Why?" Iggy had visions of patient abuse entering unheard-of realms. Ernest was going to give him nightmares.

"You know that book you were reading earlier?"

"Mm-hmm?"

"Did you get to the section on female circumcision?"

"Mm-hmm? Oh no." Iggy turned onto his stomach and lay his head on his arms.

"Yeah, well, as the African people began moving to Europe and North America they had trouble finding doctors who'd do the operation on their daughters. The doctors were usually totally unfamiliar with it, of course, and they were also mostly pretty much aghast. I don't know how much you got read out there."

"Enough." Iggy felt sick.

"I read a lot about it after I found out about Ernest. It's a really gross, horrendously painful thing that they do."

"Why? What Christly reasons do they have for doing that to themselves?"

"Tradition, initiation, reasons that don't mean anything to guys like us. Girls are circumcised because their mothers and grandmothers were done before them as far back as anyone can remember. Women are supposed to be virgins and this pretty much guarantees it."

"Is anybody doing anything about this? I mean, somebody's got to be doing something about it, right?" Iggy sat straight up now with his feet hanging over the side of the bed. It was a very high bed and his feet didn't touch the floor.

"Iggy, come back. Yes. Somebody's doing something about it now. Lots of people in official-type organizations are doing things to stop it."

"What a Jesus Christly business! What about sex? How do they have sex when they do get married? Don't tell me." Iggy sat with his hands and wrists hidden between his legs.

"Well, they end up doin' it one way or another. I don't think we should talk about this anymore. You look a little green around the gills."

"Yeah, I feel a little green. I just can't believe they didn't rise up long before this."

"Well look at us! Look at neckties and high heels and having too many children."

"But this is so much worse than neckties and high heels."

"But there was a million times the pressure."

"Yeah. But they're rising up now, right? Somebody's doing something so they must have risen up."

"Yes, Iggy, they're rising up."

"You better tell me about Ernest." He lay back down.

"Yeah, well, not being your usual kind of guy, he was happy to do the operation as long as he was given lots of money. It got around that he'd do it so he got a lot of business, a little sideline to his normal practice. He'd do whatever the relatives of the poor girls desired. But Britain passed a law forbidding it. Ernest was caught and warned and caught again, and then he lost his licence. He didn't care that much really, he had enough money. But he was frowned upon in England so he came here."

"How did you meet him?"

"Oh, he just started showing up on the beach and around town and we got to talking. He was smart and we had some good conversations. None of this stuff came out at first and we became friends, not even lovers at the beginning. We just went for dinner and walks and stuff. He was no fun but he seemed wise to me and he talked about faraway places. That always gets me goin'." Iris laughed a mirthless kind of laugh.

"So how did you come to decide to move in with him?" Iggy remembered Lewis out in the yard and wished he had tied him to something.

"Well, I knew he was rich. I wanted to fall in love with him so I could be rich too."

"Did you?"

"No, of course not, but I felt comfortable enough with him to take him up on his offer of a home. I mean, it's such a great house."

"It is that."

"I was the hostess at the Pink Lady at the time so I wasn't really hauling in the bucks. I had a reasonably nice couple of rooms above Victor's Shoes, but it was so noisy and hectic living right downtown. I never seemed able to get any peace. Sometimes I'd stay up all night just so I could have that little bit of time before dawn, the only time that's ever truly quiet around here, to kind of iron myself out, you know, assure myself that certain parts of me were still there, the parts that I like." She smiled apologetically. "I guess that sounds overly dramatic."

Iggy shook his head and smiled back at her. "Hold that thought, Iris. I'll be right back." He dashed to the bathroom which looked out over the backyard. There was Lewis under the tree smiling up at Tomas, who was fastening a red collar around the dog's neck. Iggy shouted down to them and waved and Lewis leapt about with joy. Iggy flushed the toilet, ran some water and returned to Iris in the bedroom.

"Is Lewis all right?"

"Yeah, thanks. Tomas seems to have gotten him a collar and a leash. He's a really nice guy, isn't he?"

"He's a saint."

"Okay. Where were we? You were moving in with Ernest."

"Yeah," she continued. "We still hadn't had sex when I

moved in. I was kind of hoping it would never actually happen."

"But it did happen though?" What was it like, Iggy wondered, having sex with a guy in his seventies? What did he feel like, what did it feel like when his elderly hands touched her? He was extremely curious about all of that and hoped he'd be able to ask Iris those kinds of questions later. Not just yet, he didn't think.

"Yeah, it happened all right. The restaurant deal came about shortly after that and when I started to owe him big he began to make demands. Everything changed then. The sex wasn't based on love or even lust for either of us. For me it was nasty work, and I don't know what the heck it was for him. Satisfaction of very weird desires, I guess."

Iggy leapt up. "Let's get out of here for a while. We could go for a nice long walk down the beach. We could take Lewis!"

Iris stood up unenthusiastically. "How 'bout a drive? Ernest's car is just sitting there. Nobody ever uses it but it's in good shape."

"Where will we go?" Iggy never thought of there being somewhere you could actually drive to if you headed down one of the terrible roads. Life for him in Mexico had always begun and ended in this one beautiful little town with the wide ocean spreading out and away.

"It doesn't matter. Just around. I'll pack some cold drinks and stuff in a cooler." She was already heading off to the kitchen.

"What about Ernest?"

"He's dead." Iris laughed over her shoulder.

"Yeah, but don't you have to do anything or be here or anything?"

"No. I'm in mourning. I can do anything I want. Is peanut butter and jam okay?" Iris was surrounded by slices of bread. She paused to throw Iggy a set of keys.

"Why don't you go and get the car out of the garage?"

The car was a 1957 Cadillac in what appeared to be mint condition. It was a shiny red convertible. Iggy pulled out of the garage and got out to stare at it. Lewis heard the commotion and came over to see if it could involve him in any way.

"Hey, Lewis, how're ya doin'?" Iggy scratched the little dog under his collar and Lewis began a pacing routine by the car.

"Isn't it grand?" Iris came out carrying a small cooler.

"Mm-hmm. Here, let me take that. You're gonna have to drive, Iris. I don't want to be responsible. These roads could kill this car."

"Are you kidding? It's a tank. Get in. I'm happy to drive."

"Can Lewis come?"

"Oh, Iggy. Do you mind if he doesn't? I don't like dogs, to be honest, especially horrid little stinky ones."

"Lewis isn't horrid *or* stinky." Iggy checked the dog's dishes and left him with the run of the yard. "See ya later, little fella." Lewis licked Iggy's fingers and settled down again.

They headed up or down the coast, Iggy didn't know which but he guessed it must be down if the sea was on his right. The wind was so loud and the ride so bumpy that they didn't talk much. He would have preferred a walk, Cadillac or not. Iris drove like Dicky Putz. Iggy smiled at his recollection of Arthur Pointe's description of the neighbour from hell. Old Arthur. Iggy hadn't seen him for years and he guessed correctly that he'd never see him again. Arthur had been a good person. Iggy had always come away from conversations with him feeling as though all things were still possible. He should have kept in better touch but his life got in the way of things like friendship and conversation.

He was dismally conscious of the fact that a sudden lurch of the steering wheel could plunge the car over a cliff thousands of feet to the rocks below. He watched in horror as a body dove purposefully to its certain death from a cliff jutting out into the water up ahead. He turned to Iris but she seemed not to have noticed. She looked at him. "Iggy, you've turned pure white. Are you okay?"

"I saw someone dive off that cliff up ahead. At least I think I did. Maybe I imagined it."

She laughed. "I'm sure you did. That's the cliff where the divers dive. You know, the divers, the cliff divers. I thought you might like to see them."

"Oh, thank Christ." Iggy felt a little better but not as good as he wanted to feel. He felt unsafe. He hadn't come to Mexico to lose his life or be horribly maimed in a car accident. It was supposed to be an interim haven for him.

What was the matter with him that he couldn't even enjoy a simple car ride down the coast with a lovely woman who wanted to show him the sights? He made himself sick.

Iris pulled into a parking lot, spewing gravel every which way as she decided on a spot. It was a restaurant and bar with a bird's-eye view of the cliff where divers risked life and limb several times a day. They found seats by a window and ordered drinks.

A young man walked in soon after they were settled and Iris shouted out, "Roberto." Other patrons of the bar also welcomed him, calling his name and giving thumbs-up signals.

He came over to join them. "Iris, so sorry to hear about Ernest."

"My goodness, word travels fast."

"That kind of word, yes. How are you?" Roberto looked genuinely concerned. He wore a wet diving suit and was dripping onto the wooden floor. He used both his hands to push his long black hair away from his handsome face.

"Pretty good, thanks. This is an old friend of mine, Iggy Strand. You almost gave him a heart attack when you did your last dive."

Roberto laughed and offered Iggy a wet hand.

"Good Christ, Roberto. That was you?"

"Oh, this is nothing, believe me. We have the deep water here. It's the shallow-water divers further down the coast that you should wonder at."

"Well, I hope Iris'll take me back to town before I run

into any shallow-water divers. Watching you was enough for me." Iggy took a long drink of his bourbon and felt a delicious pain spread through his body. It tasted like the first time, when he was a kid at the river with Billy Crockett.

"Roberto, have you seen Heap and Honey?" Iris asked.

"Yes, I did see them. Earlier today. They were in Heap's junky old van. I wasn't talking to them, I just passed them on the road."

"What road?"

"The road to Guadalajara."

"Maybe Heap and Honey have the right idea, getting away from this place," Iris shouted above the wind. They were back in the Caddy, driving towards town.

"Maybe they had no choice."

She looked over at Iggy. Her hair blew wildly around her face. He wished she would keep her eyes on the road.

"I hope they have a plan," she said.

"I hope so too."

They drove on without speaking till Iris pulled over and stopped the car so they could hear each other's words. "Ernest deserved to die, he deserved worse than he got, but I'm worried about whoever did it."

"What do you mean? Worried like how?"

"Well, whoever did it will pay the price forever. Anyone who'd do something so violent . . . well . . . I'm not sure how a person pays, I guess there's all kinds of ways. But I have a feeling for some people, the good guys maybe, it's like giving up another whole life, one's own maybe or one's dearest love. I mean, a person couldn't just go on, could they?"

"Why are you so concerned about a murderer?"

Iris ran her hands around the steering wheel. "I guess because whoever did it did me a huge favour. It's like a gift."

"I don't think gifts look like that."

"I hope it was Honey," she continued, "because she's

already beat. I can't bear to think of what Heap would have to go through if it was him."

Iggy reached out and touched her hair, moved it away from her face. "Are you okay?"

"I don't know. I guess so. Sometimes I wish I could live inside a dream."

"Any particular dream?"

"Yeah. It's the only one I've ever had that's come more than once, more than twice even. It's always there at the back of my consciousness, the knowledge of it runs through me. I love it, it's the best thing I have."

"What's it about?"

"You're a patient man, Iggy."

He smiled. "I like hearing you talk, when you're not talking about how worried you are about murderers."

She smiled back at him. "There's not much to it really. It's so much the way I feel when I'm in it. There's a neighbourhood of old well-built homes with huge poplars in the yards. I love poplars. It's shady but there are sunny spots if you want them and the sun on the poplar leaves, wet with rain or dew, lends a lightness to it all. There are caraganas for fences and they've been trimmed with care, just like in those southern movies where everything's so well looked after, polished wood and all that stuff. My house is huge and private, at a corner where two streets meet. Usually I'm upstairs just sort of sauntering around. There are shafts of sunlight sifting through lace curtains, dust motes in the still air.

"One room is the best. It's big and all along one side there's a screened porch facing the backyard with its trees full of songbirds. Off the porch is another porch, this one not screened, and it leads right out into the trees, into the forest. I've never gone past the porches but the option's always there. The room has more than one comfortable bed with soft down quilts. It's always been summer so everything's wide open.

"I explore down the hallways to the other rooms. Each is different, with its own features. There could be a dormer window looking out on a robin's nest, an old writing desk with a lighted lamp, bookshelves and washbasins, nooks and crannies, secret panels hiding secret rooms. It's never-ending and ever-changing and I never get to spend enough time.

"Sometimes there are people but they're always vague. I never know who they are or have much to do with them. But they're good people passing the time pleasantly and they smile and are glad to see me."

"What a great dream! I wish I could go there."

"Do you get what I mean when I say it sustains me?" Iris asked.

"Yeah, I think I do. It's dreams that keep me going too. Daydreams though. My night dreams aren't usually any good. They're why I don't like going to sleep."

"What are your daydreams about?"

"Places mostly, far-away, safe places where I could go and live a life. I don't know if they exist or not or if I got to one what I'd do, or if I could actually be happy someplace, but it's what I think about. The people in my daydreams are like your night people, kind of vague and unknown, but around, behaving themselves."

"What have you been up to, Iggy? Why are you constantly watching your back?"

Iggy sighed. "Do I seem that way?" He looked over his shoulder and they both laughed.

"Yup, you do."

He decided to tell Iris that he had plenty of money without going into detail. She was curious, but not too.

"I think I could get along somewhere," he said. "I can't believe it isn't possible. There's nothing of my old life that I want to take with me. No family or friends. I mean, I think about my stuff a lot, but I'll get over that. I'm not sure where I am but I'm hopeful. There are places and people and there can be a life."

"Yes there can."

Chapter Twenty-One

"I don't have any ID."

Heap sighed, "Me neither, babe. This part isn't gonna be easy but we'll do it. If we have to leave the van and sneak over on foot, we'll get it done." He squeezed Honey's hand and she gave him a tired smile.

"I'll be glad when this part's over with," she said.

"Yeah, me too."

They tried a small border crossing a little south of Laredo. The customs man was on his own. Between the snaps and pops of his gum he asked them to step out of the car and he laughed out loud when they confessed their lack of identification.

"Heap, honey, be a darling and fetch me a bag of Thunder Crunch potato chips, will ya?"

The guard laughed again. "Wait a minute, Missy, he ain't goin' nowhere."

Heap stopped moving.

"Please, sir, I have such a craving." Honey stretched and turned, and as she did, Fisher Stubbs saw her short dress creep up to reveal the smooth white thighs. He pressed his palms against his temples and squeezed his eyes shut for a moment.

"Go on then, get your chips," he called over his shoulder to Heap.

He shoved Honey forward with his clipboard, careful not to touch the bare softness. Gagging slightly, he yanked a bottle of Coke from the icy water of a cooler.

The room was filled with a big oak desk and not much else except pictures; there were pictures everywhere.

Honey spoke. "I guess I'm not your type."

"What the fuck do you know about my type?"

The pictures were of older women with no clothes on. Their age was emphasized, the sagging breasts and wrinkled thighs were celebrated there. Young dark-skinned men fucked the women and caressed the tired old bodies with tongues and strong fingers.

Honey moved to speak again.

"Shut up! Your voice makes me sick." He spewed the words like filth and pushed the dress up without touching flesh. His hand twisted through hair, slammed the face down on the desk. He smiled. Slammed the face again and tittered into his collar. He rammed the ice-glass inside and fucked her hard, hurting hard, till the bottle was empty.

In Honey's mind she tasted slippery skin as she pictured her teeth ripping through his flesh. Then blood. She spat. She did not want this man inside her.

She wrestled the wiry arms that trapped her. "You twisted fuck," she whispered as he forced her onto her back. She didn't have a chance.

Fisher Stubbs drew his gun. It slid easily into her and Coke gushed out in a sticky mess covering the weapon and his trembling hand. He finished with her there on the hard desk and let her be.

She imagined him hurt, bleeding from the mouth, as she righted herself to join Heap.

Fisher Stubbs wouldn't let them through after that. He wouldn't let them cross the border.

As she and Heap headed southeast Honey pictured the death of the customs man, a hurtful death at her own hand.

Chapter Twenty-Two

"Ernest did you, didn't he?" Iggy saw her face and knew he had to try harder to keep the horror out of his voice.

"Yeah, he did," she whispered.

Iris pulled the sheet up to her neck and curled up in the foetal position. She became a tight impenetrable ball and all Iggy could do was tuck the edges of her sheet lightly in around her and lie quietly as close as he dared.

An hour passed, and neither of them had moved. He gently curved himself around her still form and she allowed herself to relax a little into his comfort. She cried for a long time then, and Iggy cried too, for the second time that day, but his tears came from somewhere deeper this time, somewhere beyond his own daily frustrations and his worries about incompetence and loneliness. They welled up from a fountain of grief as old as humankind, from a place beyond gender and beyond his experience of life.

Chapter Twenty-Three

Heap was sick at heart and Honey turned matter-of-fact. They would try someplace else. They drove southeast until they came to Matamoros, across the border from Brownsville.

"Let's stop, Heap; let's have some drinks and get to feeling better, okay, honey?"

"Yeah, okay; what can it hurt?"

It was a touristy town and they found a bar that made good margaritas. They ate chili rellenos and Heap was soon able to put Fisher Stubbs out of his head. Near their table a troop of senior citizens was hooting and hollering and having a gay old time. They spoke to Heap and Honey as people do when they're on vacation. They were from a mobile-home park near Brownsville and were on a bus trip for the day.

"Brownsville," said Honey. "Gosh, that's where we're headed."

"Oh yeah?" It was one of the men talking; he wore a badge that said ARNIE and then IN CHARGE underneath. "And what brings you folks to this part of the country?"

"It's my parents' twenty-fifth wedding anniversary party this evening and we wanted to surprise them," said Honey. "They think we can't come but we've got it all worked out with my sister who's organizing the party."

"Well, that's real nice, that you're going to surprise your folks like that. They're lucky to have a couple of young folks like you looking out for them."

Arnie looked at his watch and made an announcement to the group that it was time to start moving towards the bus.

Honey had produced a Kleenex and was dabbing at her moist little face. "It's just that our truck's broken down. We're gonna miss the party on account of it. We're late already," she wailed as Heap looked on in amazement.

"Well why don't ya'll hitch a ride with us, little lady? We have empty seats and we're leaving in a few minutes. You could lock up your truck and worry about it tomorrow when the party's over and you've pleased your old parents by being there on their big day."

Several of his cohorts murmured their approval. They were getting to their feet and encouraging Heap and Honey to do the same. It was agreed that Heap would tend to the van and Honey would go with the group and purchase the tickets. The bus was running, ready for the short trip to another country. Within minutes the fugitives were ensconced in a sea of white heads, accepting cookies and cups of cool lemonade from Thermoses.

It made Heap wish he were old, like the people around him; old and kind and happy, still getting a laugh out of life after all the years of work and worry. A day trip to Matamoros seemed part of a happy person's agenda. Suddenly he knew with perfect certainty that his vision of a safe life with Honey was just a pipedream. He studied her profile as she stared at the passing countryside. She hadn't spoken since boarding the bus. Heap thought he saw a tear resting on the round curve of her cheek. He blinked and it was gone.

She turned to him. "Are you all right, Heap? You're white as a sheet."

"Give the man a drink, Etta; he looks a tad iffy." It was Arnie taking charge once more.

Heap accepted another cup of the sweet lemon drink.

"Thank you, you're all so kind. I did go all-over queer there for a moment."

A few minutes passed and Heap forced his fear back down. The next time he looked out the window they were in Texas. The border guards had spoken briefly to the bus driver and waved him on through.

Chapter Twenty-Four
North

Many kilometres to the north another border had just been crossed.

"Got any citrus in there?" was the only question the customs man asked.

Lillian had been slowly walking down the south highway when a woman in a Chevy van stopped and asked her if she needed a lift. It snapped Lillian out of her reverie. She had been trying to figure out what to do, and in her desperation to talk to someone ended up thinking of her family, those she was supposed to love, but she found no comfort there.

She had walked past her dad's house earlier on, thinking she might drop in. But then the feel of the day started to remind her of Sundays when she was a kid. She stood looking clear through the house and knew how empty it was, less than a warm glass of water. Despair weakened her so that she stumbled to the end of the street and lay flat out in the park till the feeling had lessened. She couldn't wait for night, for the house to change. It was time for her to go.

She had been able to talk to her dad once, probably because they had ended up drinking buddies for a while. But that wasn't the kind of talk she needed anymore.

"Ah, yes," he would say, "the general used to compliment me on my martinis. Just the shadow of the vermouth bottle over the glass. That's the secret, Lily. Everyone should know how to make a good martini. It was *de rigueur* when I was a young soldier and no less so now, my girl," he would say, as he poured vermouth liberally into the pitcher, slopping some down the front of his crumpled shirt.

His idea of himself as an important man, smart as a whip with connections up the ass, was concocted from books and television and remnants of the past (his or someone else's). Even Lillian on a drunk found him hard to take and would find herself taking issue.

"Dad, you aren't listening to yourself, you're making a mess of the drinks."

"Yes Lily, the shadow of the bottle. That's all it takes. Here. Help yourself." He fell down into the closest chair.

"No thanks, Dad. I gotta go," Lillian would sigh.

He tired himself out with his play-acting. There was nothing real left and the manufactured person didn't work. It was built on a structure so flimsy and unsure that it collapsed in on itself daily. By the time she had her jacket zipped he would be asleep sitting up or sometimes just staring, eyes open but mind elsewhere, real gone. She would wipe the drool from his chin as a farewell gesture and let plenty of time go by before having another go.

She had hoped that as he got older and weaker and his bluster began to fade that the myths might fall away and reveal him to her but it didn't happen. He lied to make his sad small life more interesting, even to his desperate daughter. It made him undesirable as a friend.

He had let her down. He had no respect for her life. She imagined having her own kid; she was pretty sure she would treasure it. But she didn't want to take the chance.

And Lillian couldn't think about Audrey without getting irritated. Why had everything come so easily to her? Why didn't she ever screw up the way Lillian did? And why was she so fucking happy all the time?

Plus, she never got anything. She didn't get what it was

like to be hooked on dope, or sex or crying. There was no way Lillian could confide in Audrey, tell her what her life was really like. Audrey would judge her and think she was sick in the head. She wouldn't really listen, the way Lillian needed her to. She had problems, like being unable to think of a way to make a living. She couldn't talk to her sister about that. It would make her sick when Audrey would come up with her sucked-out little suggestions.

Plus, Lillian doubted that Audrey ever even felt seriously depressed. How could she talk properly to someone who had never wished she were dead? Where Audrey lived there wasn't room for suicide or homicide or even everyday-type blues. God, how she needed someone. Iggy was pretty good for a while but she got too low for him. She needed to search among the dregs to find someone to be her friend.

She looked out the window; nothing but sky and ground disappearing into each other as day turned to night. Big deal. The driver didn't ask any questions and that was okay. Lillian didn't have any answers. It felt good to be moving, that's for sure. She always felt better when she was going somewhere. Not arriving, but the journey itself. As a child she had been fond of saying she would like to be an arctic tern. She had learned that it summered in the Arctic and wintered in the Antarctic, that it covered all those miles twice a year.

Chapter Twenty-Five

Audrey felt so low after Frank left she considered getting drunk. She hadn't done so in four years. But anything she thought about for more than a few seconds ended up seeming like a stupid idea. Her ideas were too young for her, just like most of her clothes. All she wanted was Frank. She would have traded a lot to have him there beside her. But he was with his wife.

Maybe she could rustle up a bottle of Jack Daniels from someplace and drink herself happy and then think about what to do. Or she could rustle up more than one bottle and keep drinking and drinking and drinking till she got alcohol poisoning and died, like John Bonham. Then she wouldn't have to feel this way. It was bad enough feeling generally unworthy as a human being day to day, without actually behaving badly to call attention to it. She had behaved badly by sleeping with Frank.

She decided on a walk. It was dark and she could see people moving about inside their homes. She got as far as her father's house and she stood in the dark across the street. The only light was from his darkly flickering television set. She shouldn't have come. Her hollow feeling became a cavernous black hole as she pictured her father slumped there on the couch. Were they all doomed to live out their lives alone? she wondered. She wished Lillian were there, just for a moment.

Frank. Frank was a bad idea. She regretted it so thoroughly she kept having to push it back and away every time it insisted on creeping into her consciousness. She couldn't find anything good to think about.

She decided to treat her hollowness as hunger and made her way to the 7-Eleven, where she bought a carton of Caramel Cone Explosion and a plastic spoon. She leaned against a tree on a quiet boulevard, careful not to be on anyone's property, and ate her ice cream.

At the end of her street she saw Mrs. Burbage on her veranda fooling around with some pots of what looked to be herbs of various kinds. Her movements were choppy, birdlike, purposeful as she poked and watered and re-arranged.

"Hi, Mrs. Burbage. Still at it, eh?"

"Oh, hello Audrey. Yes, I like to be out here when no one else is. It's so much more peaceful."

Audrey could recall hearing horrible children taunting Mrs. Burbage in their high mean voices. She was old, her yard was overgrown and her house in bad need of repair— reasons enough to earn her the title of Witchy Woman. Her hair had once been long and wild, more suited to her title, but Audrey noticed it was now cut short almost in a brushcut, but obviously home-done, uneven and clumpy in spots.

"Yeah, I know what you mean. It's beautiful just now, isn't it?" Audrey wanted to apologize for all the meanness and thoughtlessness.

The old woman's bright blue eyes peered earnestly out at her. "You look like you could use a good night's rest, Audrey dear."

"Yeah. Some nights just aren't made for sleeping, I guess."

"Stop and have a cup of something with me."

Audrey hesitated. She had never been in Mrs. Burbage's yard and it felt strange at first, as if she were one of the nasty kids being invited into the lair of the tormented for her just desserts.

"Not if you're in a hurry," Mrs. Burbage quickly added, turning to her plants.

"No, I'd love a cup of something. Thanks."

They sat on the porch till the eastern sky showed its first inklings. A lot of time was spent in silence but they talked too, about herbs and weather systems and other moonlit nights. Then Audrey went home to bed. She had to get up for work in an hour.

Audrey would use Mrs. Burbage like she used the turtles but for different reasons. She'd call up those blue eyes and think about the invitation offered to her on that restless night. There was safety in the offerings of the old woman down the block. Mrs. Burbage's kindness pointed to a soundness in Audrey that she lost from time to time.

Chapter Twenty-Six
South

"Come with me to Scotland, Iris." They sat outside eating toasted bagels that Iggy had found in the freezer. Lewis sat with them, alert for any bits of bagel that hit the deck. The sun was at the horizon and people gathered on the shore to watch it disappear. It seemed the light changed moment to moment. The sea was almost calm; voices and laughter rose up on the night air. Iris put a taste of cherry jam on one corner of her bagel. Iggy continued, "We could look the place over, check it out. You could think of it as a holiday."

She took a small sip of lemonade.

"Or you could think of it any way you like. I don't want to push you but I'd be really glad if you came along and it might be good for you to get away. I have lots of money."

"So you say," Iris smiled.

"Sorry. I'm not bragging or anything."

"What about Lewis?" Iris reached down and the little dog licked tentatively at her fingers. She pulled him onto her lap.

"I thought you thought he was horrid and stinky."

Iris rested her cheek on Lewis' head. "Well, I was wrong. You're not horrid and stinky, are you Lewis? And anyway, even if he was, you can't just adopt someone and then leave them behind."

"I'll figure something out." Iggy looked away and his knee started jiggling in the way that knees do, till it banged into the table, jarring the plates and causing Iris to jump and Lewis to leap up.

"I can't go away just now," Iris said.

"Why not?"

"I . . . I have a daughter here. I don't think I can leave her." She looked out at the water; her face showed the strain.

"A daughter?"

"Yeah."

"Really? A daughter? Why didn't you tell me?"

"I just did, Iggy. For God's sake, this hasn't really been a normal couple of days."

"No, but a daughter. Where is she? How old is she?"

"She's twenty-three." Iris saw the look on Iggy's face. "Not twenty-four or -five Iggy, barely twenty-three. It all happened a couple of years after you left so don't go thinking she's yours. She's not."

"Where is she?"

"Here. Here in town, in the little apartment above Victor's Shoes where we lived before I moved into the house. She hated Ernest and wouldn't live here with us. I couldn't very well make her, I knew I was asking way too much. She's always sort of disapproved of me, I'm afraid."

"Why?"

Lewis jumped back up onto Iris' lap. She bent her face down to his bony head and he settled in, looking regal and proud. "You're not such a bad little guy, are ya, now that Tomas has you all cleaned up."

"Actually it was me that—"

"Not having a father never impressed her much. I wasn't going to lie to her about it so she knows that I don't even know who it was. That's better than knowing and having her search to the ends of the earth for someone who doesn't give a hoot about her. But she thinks I'm an irresponsible slut. I probably should have lied."

"Maybe. I don't know."

"We had some good years, about ten, before she started to care about my morals. When I decided to move in with Ernest she was appalled. I guess a good mother wouldn't have gone ahead and done it but I've never been one and she already seemed lost to me anyway. I let her stay on in the apartment."

"You couldn't possibly not be a good mother."

"Yes I couldn't." Iris rubbed Lewis' chest and he leaned his head back to gaze into her eyes.

"She would have been about nineteen then."

"Yeah." She gazed back at Lewis. Iggy had a fleeting wish to be gone. He thought about an old Richard and Linda Thompson song called "Hard Luck Stories." The person in the song wasn't at all like Iris but he thought about it anyway. He wanted to sing it out loud, it had a catchy melody and was really such a riot of a song. He felt himself smiling and put a stop to it at once.

"She's made out okay," Iris went on. "She's a seamstress. She works for some of the clothing shops. I never see her unless it's by chance."

"Why not?"

"She doesn't want me in her life, I know that, but I still feel I can't leave as long as she's here."

"Let's go and see her."

"Oh, Iggy. We won't be welcome. Please, let's not."

"Come on, Iris. What can it hurt?"

"Me."

"I'm sorry. Of course it can."

They heard the back door open and close and a few seconds later a young woman stood in the open archway that led into the house.

"Janis!" Iris stood up and placed Lewis down gently on his socked feet. "Come out. I was just talking about you. This is a very old friend of mine, Iggy Strand. This is my daughter, Janis."

Iggy put out his hand. She took it reluctantly and said nothing in response to his warm greeting. Her tee shirt said FISH ARE PEOPLE TOO and her shorts allowed Iggy a view of her long brown legs. They were the only things about her that reminded him of Iris, the way she had been. Her skin was naturally dark and her almost-black hair was cut so short it would have been fuzzy rather than soft to the touch. You can pretty much do what you want when you're that lovely, thought Iggy. No hair, no personality, who would care?

"Iris, you look awful," Janis said.

"Thanks."

"Who's this? What's with his feet?" Janis knelt before Lewis.

"This is Lewis. He has sore feet so Tomas made him some socks."

"Actually, it was me that—"

"I'd like to talk to you, Iris," Janis interrupted Iggy.

"Here, let me leave you two alone," Iggy sighed. "I've got some things I have to do anyway." He had worked up quite a sweat and was glad to have a few minutes to himself.

"Who the hell is he?" Janis asked her mother, not caring that Iggy wasn't out of earshot.

"I told you, an old friend."

"An old fuck you mean. How old? Maybe he's my dad."

Iris heaved a huge sigh. "Give it a rest, Janis. You said you wanted to talk to me?"

"Yeah. It's just, I heard about Ernest. I wanted to come over and be nice to you but I guess I don't know how."

"No. I guess you don't. Do you want some lemonade?"

"Yeah. Sit down. I'll get it. Do you want some more?"

"Sure."

Janis went to the kitchen, where Iggy sat at the table doing nothing. "Taking care of business, are we?"

He smiled. "I guess you caught me."

She was the kind of beautiful that caused situations that wouldn't otherwise occur, if her lips were just a little thinner or her eyes less brown. And her manner hinted at a recklessness that too many men would want to be a part of for a while before trying to change her into something they could handle, or running for the hills.

"I'm getting the old lady some lemonade. Do you want some?"

"Yes. Thanks." He had trouble reconciling her manners with her appearance. True, she was very young, but that was no excuse. He wanted to slap her into behaving herself. His dismay increased when he realized he had grown hard and wasn't going to be able to move until something changed.

She put a glass of lemonade in front of him with no ice and less fanfare. "You can join us if you like. We're not really talking about anything." She threw the tantalizing invitation over her shoulder as she walked out.

"I'll be right out." Iggy managed to shake himself right by thinking about what an asshole he was.

Iris seemed glad of his presence. She didn't bother arguing or defending herself against the barrage of nastiness that Janis aimed at her but neither did she seem hurt by it. She bided her time, past caring.

Iggy couldn't stand it but it seemed impossible for him to fight when Iris wouldn't. He wanted Janis gone but more than that he dreaded the empty space that would be left by her absence.

It was dark when she made her move.

"How did you get here?" Iris asked.

"I walked."

"Why don't you take a cab?"

"No. I want to walk."

"It's not safe. You won't be safe. Please take a cab."

"I'll be fine."

When Iggy heard himself say, "I could walk with you part of the way," it was the first he knew of his plan to do so.

"If you like."

Iggy hoped Iris didn't mind but he couldn't tell from her face. He followed her into the kitchen while Janis visited the bathroom.

"She behaves very badly towards you."

"She's not always this bad. I'm sorry."

"There's nothing for you to apologize for. I just wish I could help somehow."

"I told you she didn't like me. I wasn't kidding."

"Would it be all right with you if I tried to talk to her about it, about what bothers her so much?"

"That's very good of you. You can do what you like but don't expect much. She'll probably just get mad and go all quiet on you. You don't have to do this Iggy, walk her home I mean."

Chapter Twenty-Seven

Iris was afraid she had given away too much. After all, who was this man she had so readily let back into her life? He hadn't earned her confidence, or a place in her house where he now seemed to feel at home. It took more than twenty-four hours of kindness to do that. She wished she hadn't asked him to stay, been desperate for him to stay, after the mess that was Ernest. It made her feel weaker, not stronger, having him here. Just the way it shouldn't. How very odd that he should turn up now.

She returned to the deck and stretched out on the wicker couch with Lewis nestled in beside her. The wind had come up and the ocean sounds were a comfort to her, water sounds. She fingered bruises on her arms, pressed hard against the bone and could almost imagine what pleasure had been like.

She lay quiet, dozing. On one of her awakenings she realized what Ernest's death meant and she felt a surge of exhilaration. It turned quickly but she recognized it. Someone had freed her and she was grateful.

There was Janis to worry about but even that disappointment seemed smaller now, less crippling. Her father had come to see her at last. She wondered if Iggy knew yet. She imagined that he did, by the way he was drawn to help her. He must have seen himself there, it was so obvious to

Iris. It quite suddenly didn't matter anymore that Janis be protected from what would surely be a letdown. Nothing much seemed to matter.

She wallowed in the free feeling, thinking of Iggy, picturing him where she knew he didn't belong. He would bury his face and fingers in her hair and bite her lips till he tasted blood. He would get it right this time. He would tease her till she was weak and then kill her with his force.

She lay still on Ernest's couch where the wind and sea blew in to calm her. They lulled her and held her and stayed the night.

Chapter Twenty-Eight

"Why are you so mean to your mother?" Iggy and Janis walked through the narrow streets among the foreign revellers and local beggars.

"Why shouldn't I be? She doesn't care about me."

"I think you're wrong there; she cares a lot."

"How do you know? Who the hell are you to be asking me this stuff, anyway?"

"I'm just an old friend of Iris' who gives a hoot about what happens to her."

"A friend from when, a friend from where? Why haven't I ever met you before or even heard of you? What kind of a friend is it that's never there?"

"From a long time ago, the summer of '69, a few years before you were born, I guess."

Janis stopped breathing.

Iggy continued, "I've been back in Canada ever since. That's where I'm from, that's where my life kept me. It doesn't make me any less of a friend because I wasn't here. Distances don't have anything to do with friendship."

She stood still, unable to catch a breath. "Summer of '69," she whispered.

"Yup, it was a heck of a summer."

She peered closely into his face and said, "Let's stop somewhere, please."

They found an outdoor place just off the beach near the centre of town. It was one of the things Iggy loved most about Mexico, the way everything was so outside. Things were better outdoors.

The only other customers sat on a wooden bench against a low stone wall and were expressing themselves quite freely from their place in the shadows. Iggy chose a table and made sure Janis was facing away from the amorous couple. Their sighs and groans were audible but she seemed unaware. They ordered margaritas from the sleepy-looking waitress and Iggy put a few coins in the jukebox to drown out the sex noise.

"I'm mean to her because I don't like her. She's a lousy mother. She says she doesn't know who my father is."

"So she's human. Big deal."

He saw the lean brown arm moving between the fat white thighs. John Cougar's voice singing "Hurts So Good" whanged out at them from the box. He hadn't punched that Christly song, had he?

"Why did you come to see her now, after all this time?" Janis asked.

"I just happened to be here. It wasn't connected with her. I didn't even know she was still here till I ran into Heap Huggins. It was just a glorious surprise and as it turns out it's a tough time in her life."

"It's always a tough time in her life. She's one big hard-luck story. Haven't you noticed?"

"She seems to have had her share of trouble, that's for sure." Iggy wondered how much Janis knew.

"Like having me, you mean?"

"No, that's not what I mean at all."

"It's because of me that she's never gotten married."

"Why on earth would you say that?"

The woman's cry could be heard even above the music. The bartender walked over and got their attention by putting his shoe between the woman's bare feet and moving her legs a further foot apart. She paid it no mind, seemed to welcome the movement. But the man took offence and after some harsh words escorted his date from the bar. The woman, who looked like an American tourist, smiled apologetically at Iggy as she passed but he averted his eyes.

"Well, nobody wants a woman with a kid, do they?"

Iggy gingerly touched his tongue to the salty rim of his glass.

"Well? Do they?"

"I don't know. Yes. Lots of men marry women with kids. I mean, they do."

Janis walked over and stuck a coin in the jukebox. She sat back down.

"Nothing's your fault, you know. Nobody thinks anything's your fault." Iggy was tired. "This is nonsense," he added. He was tired of these two unhappy women.

"How do you know?"

"Know what?"

"How do you know that nobody thinks anything's my fault?"

"Because she talked to me about you and the only things that came out of her mouth were loving things and sad things."

"Really?"

"Yeah."

"You must be good friends for her to talk to you like that."

"Well, we were once, we were in love with each other once, but I don't quite know what we are now. We only met again yesterday and so much has happened since then. It's unbelievable."

Iggy felt very unusual. The drinks were a bad idea. They tripped their way down the beach a ways before turning onto the crooked streets that led to Victor's Shoe Rebuilders. It was dark outside but the sea was alight with silver from the small moon and zillion stars. Iggy was amazed that the world could be so dark and so light at the same time.

They looked at the samples of Victor's work in the window and Iggy told Janis a story about a friend back home who wore a built-up shoe. He described how Arthur worried about being without it for one reason or another and how he owned many pairs and kept them all over the place just in case. By now he may be regretting leaving a pair with me, thought Iggy.

Janis laughed at his tale. "He must be nuts to worry that much about his shoes."

"Maybe, in his way, but aren't we all when it comes down to it?"

Janis had stopped laughing and Iggy wanted it to happen again. He wanted to be responsible for gaiety in her face. Her beauty was easier to bear when she was laughing; he didn't feel so diminished next to it.

"Are you fucking my mother?"

"What the fuck kind of question is that?"

"Just a regular one. Are you?"

"It's none of your Jesus Christly business. I can't believe you asked me that."

"Why?"

"Because it's rude. You're rude. You've got terrible manners."

"Sorry." She started up the stairs and stopped. "You're different from Iris' other friends. You're easy to talk to and not boring. Do you want to come up for a drink before going back? Are you going back there tonight?"

"I guess I am. Thanks, but I don't think I should have another drink." He felt jittery and breathless.

"Well, how about some coffee or cocoa or water or something?"

"Water sounds good."

"Come on up then."

They climbed the stairs that led up the outside of the two-storey building. The landing led into a wide screened porch. He sat back on the huge couch and closed his eyes while she went to get drinks. The warm wind blew through the screens, bringing the smell of ocean with it. He was asleep immediately and woke up a short time later only because she was kneeling between his legs sucking him gently. His fingers were in her hair pulling her to him as he came inside the small warm cave that was her mouth.

Her large breasts were pushed up by something that was invisible under them, her nipples bare and hard as she brushed them across his open lips. He felt himself getting hard again and she moved down his body to place him between her sumptuous breasts. Her fine rhythmic motion surrounded him and slowly, slowly he came again.

She washed them clean with a warm cloth.

She wouldn't let him touch her, stopped his hand as it tried to move between her legs. He wanted to enter her, it was wrong that she wouldn't let him.

"No, Pops, it wouldn't be right."

"What?"

Janis lifted one of her heavy breasts and Iggy felt the very core of him turn to ice when he saw the small birthmark there, shaped like a question mark, the same one that women had been kissing all his life, the one that Iris had kissed twenty-five years before. Iris. Ice turned to fire in his chest, a blinding searing heat, easing off to nothing.

Chapter Twenty-Nine
North

Arthur's bed was by an open window. It was almost as good as sleeping outdoors. Early Monday morning when first light caused tentative peeps and chirps to edge their way into his consciousness he felt the breeze touch his face. It brought the scent of the moist clean earth and with it memories of other springs, all springs.

He stretched and congratulated himself on his sleeping arrangements. And he took comfort from the knowledge that the earth remained strong enough, at least in his little neck of the woods, to present itself to him in this way. And it produced fruit and flowers and vegetables for him that were good and strong and disease-free. And on this morning at least, it was what woke him, finally. How very satisfying that was!

Arthur entered the cool blue morning with barely a ripple. He had been awake for almost a minute before he remembered that he had made a very grave error.

Chapter Thirty

Audrey phoned in sick. She knew her supervisor would be ordered to "deal with her" because of it, but she woke up thinking, Sometimes you gotta say what the fuck.

After she got the dreaded phone call over with she remembered that it was garbage day. The best that could happen was that Dicky Putz' garbage would be strewn willy-nilly, but even then, some part of it could end up in Audrey's yard and she'd have to handle a wretched pork chop sucked dry not only by dogs, but by Putz himself. The worst was if her own garbage with all its secrets and weirdnesses was exposed for all to see.

She felt so miserable. Maybe it was something physical. After feeding Craig and drinking her first cup of coffee she phoned her doctor only to find he was no longer in the business. The woman on the phone didn't know the inside dope or at least she wasn't letting on. This was a blow. Dr. Wiggins was the least judgmental person Audrey had ever known. He was very much in favour of things straying from the norm. When she had told him about how she sat in trees as high up as she dared for hours on end he had been filled with admiration. He was the only person she had told besides her ex-husband Terence, and he had looked at her as though she were insane.

The receptionist gave her some names but Audrey

didn't feel up to trying any of them. She had a day out of time. If only she felt like doing something, like working on the basement. She felt like a sick and empty vessel but no matter what she put inside herself it wasn't right.

The phone rang.

"Hi Audrey." Frank sounded relaxed and happy.

"Hi Frank." Audrey wished she had let her answering machine kick in.

"I thought maybe I could give you a ride to work."

"I'm not going. I'm sick."

"Really?"

"No."

"What?"

"Well, I'm not really sick but I got no sleep and I'm too depressed to move."

"Why?"

"I don't know. I've got to go, Frank."

"Does this have anything to do with you and me?"

"No." She wished she hadn't said she wasn't going to work. Now he would want to see her.

"Can I drop by?"

"No."

"Audrey, what's going on? Did something happen? Is Lillian there or something?"

"No. Nothing's going on. I just feel really horrible. We shouldn't have done it."

"Done what?"

"It."

"Oh."

Frank was quiet and Audrey stared at the picture of her and Lillian on the fridge. They looked so happy. A pleasing memory stirred inside her but she couldn't quite catch it.

"Why?" asked Frank. "What about all that stuff you said about no one being unfaithful and everything?"

"I was wrong." The feeling was gone and Audrey was left staring at a faded photograph of two wholesome-looking strangers laughing into each other's faces.

"Oh no!"

"Frank, for Christ's sake. Grow up! Sorry, I didn't mean that."

"Yes you did."

"No, I didn't. I'm really sorry. Look, I think I just feel really depressed. It's probably independent of anything you and I did. Maybe it's hormonal or something. I just want to spend the day alone."

"I think we should talk about this in person. It's no good on the phone."

"Please Frank. I'm going to hang up now. I'll talk to you later, okay?"

"Okay."

All she could manage after hanging up was to drag herself back to bed. She dreamed she was cleaning the basement and she came upon her mother there in a small room. When Audrey asked her why she had left the family home so long ago she said it was because she hadn't particularly liked having children. It hadn't turned out the way she'd pictured it. And when Audrey asked her why she was there now in her basement of all places, she said, "This is where they put me. Ironic, isn't it?" And she laughed then, a distant unknowable laugh.

Chapter Thirty-One
South

Iris knew the moment she awoke. All else disappeared and was replaced by this new fact in her life. If only she had told him. She was going to, later, if there was a later. But it hadn't even occurred to her that he would sleep with their daughter.

They would find out if they didn't know already. That sweet spot that had shown up so splendidly on the chest of her baby daughter. Iris had laughed when she first saw it and kissed it as she had kissed the father's. When she had first seen it on Iggy it seemed to her that she recognized it, it was so familiar already.

Now she saw the rest of her life stretched out before her like a dusty grey road and wondered what she would do with all that time. In the hours while she slept she had lost the last thing she had to lose, something to do with hope. She wouldn't be able to hope anymore.

Surely he would have the sense not to come back. She didn't think she could stand to see him again. Or her, especially her.

He had remembered what she took in her coffee. She shouldn't have thought that was important, it wasn't. Things like that weren't. The look on his face when he first saw her again didn't have anything in it to warn her of what he would do. It was cruel what they did, it was the worst thing, but Iggy wouldn't see it that way. Janis would, but that didn't hurt as much. Iris didn't expect more from her.

She had slept on the deck waiting for Iggy to return. The morning was cloudy and cool and she was grateful for that. She stood and leaned against the rail, into the wind. It blew against her, through the heat of her realizations. Her greatest desire was for people, for everyone, to leave her alone. She didn't want to talk or have anyone look at her.

Lewis stirred as well, but kept his distance, working quietly at his socks on a far corner of the deck.

Iris thought about how she would phone Ernest's lawyer and see if she could finish with that business. Maybe he could close the restaurant for a while—pay the workers, see to the perishables, put up a sign, all that. Then she could lie on the couch and look out to sea. Before long people would understand that she didn't want to see them. It was something to strive for, something small that couldn't be confused with hope.

She heard someone at the back door but it didn't occur to her to answer it. Soon there was a man standing in the sand looking up at her. It took her a moment to realize it was the policeman who had been there the day before. He reminded her of the head cop on *Miami Vice*, the one with the quiet way about him, the captain.

"Sorry to bother you, Ms. Blowers."

She noticed the gentleness of his voice; it was pitched in an agreeable key. Lewis was alert but busy with his feet. Two socks on, two off.

"I'm afraid I have more bad news for you." He came up the wooden stairs to where she stood.

She was puzzled. Since when did police deal in crimes of the heart, betrayals by family members and old friends. She was so tired. Couldn't he see she needed to sleep, that his presence wasn't necessary? She already knew what he had come to tell her.

" . . . no pain, we're almost certain."

"What, what was that? Sorry."

"I was just saying we're almost certain he didn't suffer at all. It was quick."

Relief sluiced slowly through her when she realized that Iggy's death was the cause of his not coming back to her. Then, in answer to her questions, the soothing voice took that relief away again as it reluctantly described the scene above Victor's Shoe Rebuilders. Her questions stopped then and the policeman came to the point of his visit.

"We're trying to find out who to notify about this. We don't even know where he was staying." Then, carefully, "Was he staying here with you?"

By now the practised tact and kindness of the policeman were wearing on Iris. She wished he would rip her to shreds with a blundering cruelty that matched his words. She wanted to be left for dead.

"I don't know where he was staying. I don't know if he has any relatives. I didn't know him very well. Please go now."

"Yes, all right. Sorry." He started slowly down the stairs.

"Officer?"

"Yes." He turned back hopefully.

"Where's my daughter?"

"Who?"

"My daughter, the girl who was with him."

The policeman blanched. "Oh. I'm sorry. I didn't know. Her name, it—"

"She chose her own name."

"She's at home. Up above—"

"Yes. I know where she lives."

Lewis limped over to where Iris had sat down on the couch and rested his head on her thigh. She didn't notice but he stayed anyway till midday when she got up and went into the house.

The first thing she saw when she woke up the next time was a room key for the Pink Hotel. It sat on her night table where Iggy had left it along with his wallet and other sundries from his pockets. She opened the wallet. Paul Syms. Ah yes. She had no intention of phoning the police with the information, she had no intentions at all, so was surprised when she found herself in the hotel lobby a short while later.

She took the elevator to the sixth floor and found his room. It was unruffled. The police hadn't found it, they probably weren't even looking. There wasn't much to go through, some clothes hanging neatly in the closet and folded in drawers, a couple of near-empty suitcases, bathroom accoutrements lined up on the sink. It didn't take her long to find what she was looking for, the passport and the safety deposit box key. They were the only identifiers in the room.

Chapter Thirty-Two

The Gulf air, clean and salty, came at her in a rush. She had noticed a hint of it back in Houston but now its warmth was all around her, pushing her down the beach, causing her to laugh out loud with its rambunctiousness. Lillian felt something that she didn't recognize at first. It filled her up and moved inside her in an old familiar way. It was joy of course, pure and simple.

Chapter Thirty-Three
North

Audrey lay down on the grass and looked up at the sky. She often did so, sometimes even in the winter when the ground was covered with snow. As children, Audrey and Lillian used to lay in the soft grass and chew on the plump white ends, clean from the earth. They gazed up at the deep blue and drove themselves crazy with the idea that it never ended. Now Audrey thought about Frank. He had been there while she slept and left a note. It said:

> Audrey, what's going on? I can't believe that you
> regret what happened. It was all so great. You
> weren't wrong about anything. You were right!
> Maybe we could go to a drive-in tonight, or at
> least out for a milkshake. Come on Aud. Call me.

She was sorry now that she had missed him and sorry about the way she had talked to him on the phone. She wished more than anything that he would come back now and be with her. But she couldn't pursue this, he belonged to another family.

It was late Monday afternoon when Arthur came over. Em was doing her papers on the other side of the lane. Down one side, up the other. She took the precaution of putting them in plastic. Environment Canada hadn't predicted another storm but it was coming. It was a sweltering day, 34 degrees the last time Audrey looked at her window thermometer.

Arthur was distraught and it took some doing on Audrey's part to get him to tell her what was wrong. They started out on the porch but were driven inside by Dicky Putz, who was in his garage with the radio turned up loud. It was tuned to a religious station and a fervent disciple hollered over the air waves that yes the time had come, the time had come today. It sounded comical to Audrey, it reminded her of an old Chambers Brothers song. But it was more than Arthur could stand. They went inside and Craig jumped on Arthur's lap as soon as he was settled. That seemed to comfort him and he began to talk.

"I've made a very grave error, Audrey."

"What do you mean?"

Arthur licked his lips and concentrated on Craig's ears. The cat purred and began puffing little bursts of air out the sides of his mouth.

"It's a case of mistaken identity, you might say."

"Arthur, what are you talking about?"

"I'm talking about something that I did on Saturday morning."

Saturday morning. Saturday morning. Audrey had seen Arthur Saturday morning lying in his hammock and puttering around his yard.

He began to shiver and Craig leapt from his lap and went to sit next to Audrey's only cactus.

"Arthur, it couldn't be that bad. What could you possibly have done that would make you such a wreck?"

"I killed the wrong man."

"What?"

"I killed someone on Saturday morning and it wasn't the person I intended to kill."

Audrey's head felt like it was being squeezed in a vice. This was life-altering information, news that would change everything. She sat down on the footstool. "Arthur, what are you talking about?"

"I trusted him with my shoes and he used them to smuggle hash oil into the country. He threw one of them away. He used it and then he threw it in a dumpster. Kenneth found it. My shoe was used to smuggle drugs and then it was thrown away."

"Who did this?"

"Nate Underhill. He hollowed out the big shoe and filled it up with contraband."

"Nate Underhill? Who's Nate Underhill?"

"An acquaintance of mine."

"How do you know he did this, Arthur?"

"Kenneth brought me the shoe and I recognized it as one of the pair I kept at Nate's place."

"So you killed him?" Audrey tried to keep the hysteria out of her voice. She was frightened at what she thought of as her own stupidity. How could she not have known that one of her best friends was insane? She snatched Craig away from the cactus, where he was getting prickly little spines embedded in his nose.

"No. That's just it. Apparently I killed someone else, someone named Henry Gladue. It's in this morning's paper. It was an innocent person that I killed."

Nate Underhill. Ignatius Strand. What was going on here? wondered Audrey. Had this new Nate person lived with Lily and Iggy, or did he even exist, or were he and Iggy the same person, or . . . what!

"Arthur, you have to go to the police. They're after the Purse brothers for that murder."

"Don't worry about them. The police won't be able to make anything stick. I did it."

"It doesn't matter. You have to see them anyway. I'll go with you. We could phone Frank," she added brightly.

The thin walls of Audrey's house were no match for the blast of Dicky's radio. Arthur put his hands over his ears as he stood up.

"I'm going to tell that man a thing or two. I can't take it

anymore, Audrey. It's time I stood up to him."

"Arthur, maybe this isn't the time. You're so upset."

"What better time?" He moved woodenly toward the door and she didn't try any harder to stop him. She did follow him, though, as far as the end of her sidewalk, so she could keep an eye on the confrontation. She had a strong desire to protect the insane murderer who had been a good friend to her for so many years.

Huge dark clouds moved in quickly from the west, distant rumblings as she watched him lurch awkwardly toward his foe. The smell of ozone mingled with the fumes of propane from someone's outdoor barbecue. Too much propane. It was as though they had turned on the gas and then forgotten to light it, so it was collecting up and collecting up. Looking over to the Putz yard, Audrey saw that the barbecue was set up inside his garage. Stupid man! Dicky was sauntering toward the entrance with an unlit cigar in his mouth and his hands working with a box of wooden matches. She knew instantly that it was too late to save anyone.

Arthur turned around and smiled back at her. "Looks like it's coming up to quite a storm," he shouted, and waved as though he knew it was goodbye.

Her calling of his name was lost in the explosion that blew both men high into the blackening sky.

Arthur had been right to fear Dicky Putz, but in a way Putz had saved him.

Chapter Thirty-Four

Audrey stood by the open grave. Her old black umbrella did a poor job of warding off the wet. Water trickled down the collar of her cream-coloured suit. The sky was solid grey, like a West Coast winter. She had tried the coast but couldn't get used to the leaden season. Some days she had thought she might suffocate in the gloom.

She trembled in the cold of the summer rain. She wanted to speak to the stiffly standing couple on the other side of the gaping hole but it seemed impossible. Aunt Joan and Uncle Len. There were few other mourners, and she wondered at the small circle of acquaintances of such an interesting man.

As she thought about her friend she tried again to compute the facts of Monday afternoon. She didn't yet look behind the information, just saw the events lined up in the order in which they happened, no overlapping, no shady areas; they were two-dimensional for now.

Arthur's death made everything different. It was an imprecise thing but Audrey could feel it, a sea change within herself. Her daily life went on much as before; it had more to do with what was possible and what no longer was. Frank fell into the latter category. He was lost to her as surely as if it were he who had been blown to kingdom come.

He was her first lover and her last. She had thought about him even during the years when she seldom saw him, just imagining him being a cop or a dad or a husband, a guy she loved. It had always been okay with her that she couldn't have him. She had known he was there and that he had loved her and very likely still did. She had never imagined this new time together and wondered now if she had invented it.

She began to wonder too at the circumstances that placed Arthur at Putz' place just in time for the explosion. It was so close to her physically that she began to go over the ways she could have prevented it. It would have been easy for her to hold herself accountable but she forced herself not to, she gave herself that gift.

Audrey's world grew small after Arthur and Frank disappeared from her life. Each morning she hauled herself from sleep in time to catch the early bus. She did her job and came home. If people spoke to her she tried to pay attention to what they said, and answer them.

"So Audrey, any big plans for the weekend?"

"No, not really." She tried to smile, she didn't want them thinking she was weird.

"Looks like it's gonna be another wet one anyway."

"Better wet than never" was her response. Her co-worker laughed and walked away. Did I say something funny? Audrey wondered. Did I say anything at all? She walked home on the days when it wasn't raining. There weren't many of those. She wanted to tire herself out and she did.

Her small world was practically enough. Her dreams ran parallel to her daily life, keeping her alive. Sometimes the desire to dwell only in dreams became so strong it got her into trouble. Like when her old friend Hilda came to pick her up for a night out and found her lying in the grass looking up at the sky. She had forgotten, and didn't even remember when Hilda reminded her. Twice, she did that.

So she spent a lot of time alone so she didn't have to work so hard.

She was amazed at how much she missed Frank. It had been only two days of loving him again. Surely she could get over it. She wanted to hear him talk and watch his face as she talked, and she wanted to lean back while he kissed her neck, and forward as he kissed her back, there on her grandfather's dusty couch.

He left messages, and came over twice, but she wouldn't answer the door. He mentioned Arthur on the phone but she didn't want to hear that name. It sounded tinny and small when he said it. He thought she might want to talk about the explosion but she didn't. She lived next door to it, she witnessed it, that was enough.

Some people share death generously as they would summer raspberries when they have more than enough for themselves. They talk easily of their loss and receive their special treatment gratefully, matter-of-factly. Death makes them special for a time and they notice the people who tend to them. Others hold it tightly to their chests, not wanting to let it out of their grasp in case someone should trivialize it with kindness. It is too big to share. Audrey knew Frank wanted to help, he was a compassionate man who listened to people when they spoke, weighed what they said carefully. At the same time he didn't press himself upon people. He knew there was nothing to be gained by doing that. It was better all round to allow for things. He was an innocent man, a good man, and it wasn't long before he understood that he should leave her alone.

Chapter Thirty-Five
South

They all had jobs. Heap worked in the harbour loading and unloading boats. No one there cared who he was or where he came from. He was big and strong and easygoing and he worked hard. He had the chance to take short trips but didn't want to leave the two women.

It was a touristy sort of place and felt right to the three of them. Honey had no trouble finding work as a cocktail waitress. One place was pretty much the same as another. They all had men who reacted to her the way she used to think she wanted them to, the way they always had. Heap worried about her all day while he worked and all night while she worked, but she always came home and she still seemed to want him around.

It had taken Lillian longer to find work because it hadn't occurred to her to look. She had been on the beach as usual when she got talking to a man who took an interest in her. He listened while she described her trip south and the feelings and circumstances of a life that led her that way. He smiled at her and encouraged her to be frank. She felt good talking to him and was thrown for a loop when two men dressed in white apprehended her new friend and put him in the back of a van belonging to the state mental hospital. He was an escapee.

This was before Heap and Honey so she had time on

her hands. She found the hospital and hitchhiked out to visit Whit, as he had called himself. He was the only Whit so it wasn't hard to track him down. She went often and got to know some of the other patients as well, told them stories, seemed to know what kinds of things they could stand to hear without getting upset. They looked forward to her visits, as did members of the staff, who appreciated the time she spent and saw how the patients perked up when she walked into a room. She was a bit like a volunteer worker, the best they'd ever had. They offered her a job, they didn't want to lose her.

Lillian thought it was a miracle. Her job was to visit with the patients, it was what she wanted. There was the worry that she would ruin it somehow but not for a while, she was on a roll. She was able to see clearly into the confusion of people's minds, through it to their centres, connecting with them there and offering herself to them like a sturdy live branch to swing on. Sturdiness was new to her.

She didn't reach everyone of course, the place was vast with countless levels of illness, but she was allowed to travel as far as she liked. Whit's ward was her favourite. They loved her there, Whit most of all, and she had no wish to argue with that.

Chapter Thirty-Six

The road to Guadalajara could lead anywhere, it was the main road out of town. So Roberto the deep-water diver's information about where they had last been seen wasn't really much of a clue. Iris wanted to find them, Honey in particular, to let her know about Ernest's will. He had left her very well off.

Iris reopened her restaurant in the fall. It was a surprise when she woke up one day longing to be back at her place of business on the beach. She lay in bed and imagined it, pictured herself moving from room to room keeping an eye on things. She smelled the prawns on the grill and the simmering herbs in the cast-iron pot. In the bar she heard the quiet breaking of the waves past the murmurings of her customers. She couldn't wait to get back there! Some things would change, the name of the place for one. And she would do without the flowers. Maybe she'd get a piano.

Janis was around. Iris had seen her twice but they hadn't spoken. Iris wouldn't leave her but neither was she ready to try again. She knew the time would come but she was going to wait this time, let it happen to her. Not to say she wouldn't be the one to make the first move but she wasn't going to rush in. There was time. Iris felt it, felt comfortable about her relationship to time, the way it had slowed for her and let her enter.

In the dream she had been scared at first, clipping along in a small craft on the rolling brown waves. There were obstacles to be avoided. They weaved in and out and it took her a few moments to understand that the driver was doing a fine job. She realized then that she was with a friend, an old and trusted friend, so she could relax and enjoy the wild ride. She hadn't known about this special skill that her friend possessed but she didn't question it now. The water rolled above them and willingly parted to allow for the antics of the little boat. It was as good as flying.

Then they were in a log establishment where men were. There was a man she wanted to kiss. Everything about him, his shape, his presence, his look, pulled her to him and they fell into the kiss like the boat had taken to the waves.

Chapter Thirty-Seven
North

Audrey took advantage of the clear day to hang out a load of laundry, feeling great satisfaction as she watched the steam rise from the clean clothes when she pegged them to the line. She breathed deeply and decided to spend as much of the day outside as she could. The insides of places had been getting to her, her allergies were getting worse. She phoned one of the doctors on the list Dr. Wiggins' receptionist had given her but he wasn't taking any new patients. She recognized one of the other names as a doctor who had been charged with something indecent over the summer. Great. Good job compiling the list, Dr. Wiggins.

She raked and pulled and planted bulbs, and sat and read and stared into space, cosy under her porch quilt. More than once she went to the fence to talk to Arthur and then remembered that he was dead. She wanted to talk to him about the losses in her life. She supposed she missed him even more than Frank. He had been part of the dailiness of her life and, after all, Frank still existed. If only . . . if only . . . if only she had known Arthur was going to die. If only she had known he was going to kill someone. Someone named Henry that he thought was someone named Nate who had indeed turned out to be Iggy.

Audrey knew it could just as easily have been her, committing a murder, almost. They had been so similar in their feelings about things, in their frustrations and their far-fetched solutions. Kindred spirits. She wondered what small turn Arthur had taken in his life that made it possible for him to do what he had done. Or perhaps what turn had been taken on him that had taken such a toll. She should have paid more attention, she should have seen him more clearly.

She stopped in the park on her way home from the little store. It was a golden autumn day, warm and cool at the same time. The sun was low in the sky but she found a sunny bench and sat awhile enjoying the glorious smell of death all around her. Maybe she could find Lillian if she really tried. They could lie on a lawn somewhere and drive themselves crazy with thoughts of forever.

Audrey bought an Arctic sleeping bag. She hadn't slept indoors since the explosion and the nights were starting to get chilly. The couch on her porch had been pulled out into a bed and left that way. She couldn't imagine wanting to sleep in the house ever again. The fresh air made her feel good and she wasn't worried about winter. She could pretend it was long ago and that she had tuberculosis. She had read somewhere that TB patients slept outside, bundled up in the cold. It was a treatment of sorts.

Chapter Thirty-Eight
South

It was early spring before Iris saw Heap Huggins again. He made his way back to where the weather suited his clothes. He was thinner and sadder than when he left; Iris didn't know him for a moment. He came to her first under cloak of night to make sure no one was looking for him. She reassured him and he told her about the two women, Honey and Lillian.

"Iggy's dead. Did you know that?" They were on the deck, sipping beer.

"What?"

"Iggy. He's dead."

"What do you mean dead? How could he be dead?" Lewis had been sleeping on Heap's lap and was startled awake as his new friend leapt to his feet. "Sorry Lewis." Heap bent and lifted the dog up in his arms.

"He died of a massive heart attack."

"Where? When?"

"Here. I mean, downtown here, almost a year ago now. Actually, it was around when you and Honey left, around when Ernest died, about exactly then. God, sometimes it seems like everyone's dead."

"Well, Jesus. What next? He didn't even belong here.

He shouldn't have died here." Heap sat back down with Lewis on his lap staring at him.

"Is he buried here?"

"No. He was cremated, and, well, he's in the greenhouse."

"In the greenhouse? He's here in your home?"

"Well, he's out back in the greenhouse." Iris reached over to scratch the dog's ears. "Iggy found old Lewis here, didn't he little fella?"

"What about his people?"

"Whose people?"

"Iggy's people, he must have some people somewhere. He came from Canada. He must have someone up there." Heap got up again and started to pace. Lewis fetched his rawhide and settled in on top of Iris' feet.

"Can I see him?"

"See him?"

"Yeah."

"There's nothing to see really. It's just a can, like a small paint can with a handle, you know, nothing much to look at."

"Did you have a service?"

"A service! Heap, for Christ's sake, what are you going on like this for? No one knew him here. All there was was me. I took his ashes, I kept his ashes, but no, I didn't have a service."

"Well, at least you've got his ashes. Did you try to find his people?"

"No. Heap, I'm very tired. Could you please go? Come back tomorrow if you like."

"Sure Iris. Sorry." Heap took a last swallow of his beer and gave Iris a quick kiss on the cheek. "Have a good sleep. I'll see you in the morning. See ya, Lewis." Lewis' shortened tail made whapping sounds on the wood.

Chapter Thirty-Nine

Eight hours later Heap stood at the sliding glass doors leading in from Iris' deck.

"Good morning, Iris. I was wondering if I could see Iggy's ashes now." Lewis cavorted briskly around Heap's feet. "Good morning, Lewis." He leaned down to give the dog a friendly pat.

"Sure, Heap. Come on in, I'll get the key. I'm sorry I was short with you last night." Iris was fresh from the shower.

"Not to worry. I like your hair cut short like that. It perks you up some."

She smiled, "Thanks, Heap. Yeah, I like it too, it's part of the new me." She laughed as they headed out the back way.

They crossed the damp grass to the greenhouse, where Iggy's ashes sat on the top shelf of a free-standing cupboard. The building had been cleared of all live things.

"Iris"—Heap held the ashes in his two big hands—"I was wondering what you'd think of the idea of me taking Iggy's ashes north."

"North?"

"Yeah, north to Canada, to the place where he came from. I'd like to take him home. Someone there should know that he's dead and I'd like to make the trip. I've got nothing planned and I'm getting real good at crossing borders," he grinned.

Iris smiled back at him. "Well, Heap, I think it's a good idea. You're probably right about him having some people somewhere, and even if you can't find them you could scatter him someplace nice. He talked about two rivers that met near the place where he lived."

"Great! Thanks, Iris. I'm real glad you think this is a good idea. I'm gonna leave today."

She walked him to the road. He looked like a big kid hanging on to his lunch pail. "You're a good one, Heap. I hope I see you again. Good luck." She reached up and kissed him.

"Thanks, Iris. You take care now, and I'll be seeing you."

Chapter Forty
North

Audrey's Vasque walking boots crunched down on the uneven patches of ice as she made her way to the bus stop. The city ploughs had ignored her neighbourhood this year and the streets were a mess now that melting season had begun. By the time she came home in the early afternoon the lane would be a lake and she would hop from ice island to ice island in an effort to protect her feet. She needed a good pair of boots for this weather. It never lasted long so she tended to put it off from year to year as an unnecessary expense. Her Vasques were fine boots but not meant to be abused in this way.

It was getting light in the east. The first hints of it had appeared in mid-February as she stood waiting for the 6:38. What a lift it gave her! Maybe that was what was wrong with her, lack of daylight hours. She could start getting better now.

She shivered as she waited for the bus. A turtleneck or a scarf would have been a good idea. And her legs were cold. She shouldn't have put her long underwear away just yet. But there was no wind and the birds were singing ferociously. Things could be worse.

The bus didn't come. It had happened before so Audrey wasn't surprised but she felt the heat of her anger in her chest as she plodded her way over the bumpy ice to Main

Street. She tried not to care that she would be late. Her right foot went through some thin ice covering a pothole and the water came up over the top of her boot.

"Fuck!"

She was tempted to turn around and head back home but she kept on. A picture of herself in a long flannelette nightgown and woollen socks danced behind her eyes, and her couch, and her quilt of soft down.

As she approached the lights of the main thoroughfare she saw a bus pull away from the stop. The driver saw her and she waved frantically to no avail.

"Prick!"

She sat down on the bench and took some deep breaths. Her foot was freezing. A car stopped and offered her a lift. Why not? she thought. If he rapes and kills me at least it will be something different in my life. She realized then that she didn't care if she lived or died.

The driver turned out to be the nice man who was sometimes on the same bus with Audrey. He had gone home for his car when it hadn't come. She pretended she had known it was him so he wouldn't think her behaviour suspect. Why did she care what he thought? Why would she still care what strangers thought of her when she didn't care if she lived or died?

The man sympathized with her over her foot and dropped her at the employee entrance to her building. Her supervisor wasn't in the immediate vicinity so she just pretended she forgot to punch in. After getting things underway at her desk she went off to her locker to change into her shoes. She was sure she had an extra pair of thick socks in there somewhere.

"Ahh. . . ." If she were dead she wouldn't know the deep comfort of drying her wet frozen feet and placing them gently into soft woolly socks. She put on her dry shoes and sauntered back out to work. She wouldn't hurry, she wouldn't let it get her down.

After a few minutes at her desk she ran the fingers of both hands through her hair. "It's so fucking hot in here," she said out loud to no one in particular.

Two of her male co-workers looked nervously at her and then at each other. She wondered if they hated her. She considered walking out then and not coming back, shaving her head, getting on a Greyhound going south. After a while her hair could grow back and she could start again. It would be fun to watch it grow.

Audrey wanted a clean slate. She was so tired of her worries. They bored her and made her feel inferior because they were trivial and she still couldn't handle them. She wanted to go to bed at night with a clear conscience but she didn't know how because she wasn't clear about the things that filled her with the infernal guilt. Any unpleasantness in her life seemed to worm its way into a black pool of negativity deep within her, add itself to the dark swirling waters of what she interpreted as incompetence and regret.

When she got home from work Frank and Big Heap Huggins were sitting on her porch waiting for her. Frank had had an idea that Audrey might be interested in meeting him. The first thing Heap saw when he walked into Audrey's kitchen was a picture of Lillian on the fridge.

When Audrey described this year of her life to people later on, the word 'coincidences' often came up. She didn't know it till then but she didn't believe in that word. Series of events and thoughts and instincts led to things. They didn't come out of nowhere. There were layers and layers of them, all there to be found, all existing at once, if anyone chose to devote a lifetime to finding the patterns.

Chapter Forty-One

It was Frank's day off so Audrey decided to walk by his house on the off chance. He was in his yard working around, with a young child playing nearby. When he saw her he stopped and smiled. "Hi, Audrey."

"Hi, Frank."

The kid came over immediately when she saw something sociable was happening. Frank put his hand on her shoulder. "This is Sadie. Sadie, this is Audrey, an old friend of mine."

"Hello. My mum's in the Chemical Withdrawal Unit again and in the summer I'm going to day camp."

"Oh. Well, hello Sadie."

Sadie, at four and a half, didn't miss the look Audrey gave Frank when she heard the information about Denise.

"We deal with it by talking about it. We think that's best," she said.

"I'm sure it is best, Sadie. It's always good to talk about things." Audrey crouched and leaned against the chain-link fence.

"That's what we think."

"Audrey, would you like some lemonade? Sadie and I were just about to take a break."

"Well . . ." Audrey did want to tell Frank her plans.

"Come on. Come in the house."

"I can't."

"Sure you can. Come on in, Audrey."

"No. I mean I can't. I'm attached to your Jesusly fence."

Sadie looked at her dad and said, "Audrey said 'Jesusly.'"

Frank laughed. "Audrey, Audrey, Audrey. Here, let's see if we can get you disattached. Think we should, Sadie, or should we just leave her here for a while?"

Sadie danced a jig around the yard, making small hooting sounds.

"Why would you have a horrible fence like this around your place anyway?" Audrey asked.

"Don't ya like it?" Frank freed Audrey and tousled her hair.

"It's downright dangerous," she said.

Sadie shrieked with hilarity as the three of them headed into the house.

They led Audrey into a little sunroom off the living room. Sadie's cutouts were spread out over the floor and a bulky old tabby was lying upside down in the last available sunbeam.

Sadie sat down in front of an untried page of Counsellor Troi's outfits.

"What's your cat's name?" Audrey asked.

"Byron."

"He's grand."

"Yup, he's a good old boy, all right." Frank rubbed his stomach and Byron stretched out long.

"I'll go get us that lemonade."

"I've got a cat at home who looks about Byron's age. How old is he, Sadie?" Audrey rubbed his ears as he purred in ecstasy.

"Twenty-two. He's named after a poet."

"Wow! Twenty-two, eh? He's in great shape. You must take really good care of him. My Craig is seventeen. I thought that was old."

"Craig?"

"Yes. That's my cat's name. He's a striped lout just like Byron."

"May I come and see him?"

Audrey hesitated. "Sure you can." She saw the doubt in Sadie's eyes and moved on. "Cutouts, eh? I used to love doing cutouts." She was reminded of some she'd had when she was a kid, Juliet Jones and her sidekick, the admirable Eve with her wild white hair and extravagant gowns.

Sadie said, "Would you like to see Counsellor Troi's new outfits?"

Audrey leapt at the chance and was on her knees, scissors in hand, when Frank came back with refreshments. Sadie was pleased with Audrey and took a break with the two grown-ups while they drank and passed the time.

"Yes. My dad and me and Em and Garth are very sad but we're trying our best to get on with things. How do you know my dad?"

"We went to high school together a long time ago."

"He's very sad right now."

"You're a brave girl, Sadie. I think you've got the right approach. Your dad's lucky to have you to talk things over with."

Sadie beamed.

Audrey turned to Frank. "I'm hopping on a Greyhound with Heap."

"Yes, I thought you might."

Sadie took her drink over to her spot on the floor and busied herself with Deanna Troi's diamond tiara.

"I have to go with him, Frank. It's just, there isn't a morning I wake up when she isn't the first thing that comes to me. And there isn't a night when I turn out the light that she isn't the last thought before sleep. Just since she's been gone, I mean.

"It's got so I can't say her name out loud. I just say 'my sister.' I wish people would stop asking me about her. I haven't known how she is, or where she is, and sometimes I think they're just asking to be mean.

"I can feel her, Frank. I can feel her inside me, further

inside than I've ever been. She feels like a slow-running river or a tern caught in a slipstream, just a small motion inside me. I have to go where Heap says she is."

"I know you do." Frank covered her hand with his.

"I just want someone here to know where I've gone."

"Thanks for letting it be me, Audrey. What about work and everything, have you got it all figured out?"

"Yeah, pretty much, I think."

"What about Craig?" Sadie asked.

"I've got him pretty much figured out too, Sadie. My good friend Hilda's gonna take him for a while. She loves Craig so he'll be in good hands."

She took a last drink of her lemonade. "I've got to get going. Thanks for the drink and everything."

When Audrey was leaving, Sadie said, "Thanks for playing with me, Audrey. I'm glad you think we have the right approach."

Audrey gave her a hug. "Be sure to drop over sometime when I get back and I'll introduce you to Craig." Sadie's face lit up and to Audrey's chagrin tears came to her own eyes. Her grandfather had been like that, tearing up at the slightest thing, even in his younger days. She remembered watching *Leave It to Beaver* with him on his old black-and-white set, seeing the tears running down his face when Beaver's pet pigeon died. The tears had embarrassed him then as Audrey's embarrassed her now and she cursed her Scottish roots.

Chapter Forty-Two

They departed early on a blue May morning. They had decided to fly. Audrey felt wildly free in a way that she hadn't since the days when she used to walk out of jobs without telling anyone that she had quit. Back in the days when finding a job was as easy as skimming the want ads. This time she had taken a three-month unpaid leave of absence so she had a safety net if her inklings didn't pan out. She looked forward to the small pointed face, and was anxious too, about what Lily's reaction might be.

She remembered some words that Arthur had spoken about letting family ties get in the way, how she would probably get on better with her sister if she just saw her as another of earth's creatures struggling as best she could to get by.

"It's pretty ironic."

"What's that, Heap?"

"Well, me going all the way to Canada looking for Ig's people and then finding the most important one right back where I started from."

"Yeah, but I guess it was good his mother was told even if it didn't seem as though she got it."

"Yeah, I guess."

On the day Heap and Audrey had found Iggy's mother in the Tall Grass Mental Health Centre she had been fastened into a chair and put in front of a window facing the pouring rain. She was as thin as a human being could be and the lines in her face looked as though they would break if given an emotion to display. She looked petrified, a woman of stone. They gave it their best effort but she didn't turn to look at them when they talked and she didn't speak at all.

"How do you think Lily will take it?" Heap continued now. "Was she in love with him or anything?"

"I don't honestly know. I . . ." Tears came to Audrey's eyes and her throat closed up as she remembered how she hadn't wanted to listen, hadn't wanted to hear anything that Lily had to say.

"I'm sorry, Audrey. What is it? Did I say something?"

"No, don't worry, Heap. It's just . . . I wasn't the best sister in the world, you know."

"I'm sure you did the best you could. Don't be hard on yourself, Audrey. Sometimes people make it difficult for people to be nice to them. And some people just aren't suited to one another either."

"Thanks. Well, I've got Iggy's note to give her anyway."

Audrey and Heap were relaxed with each other by now so the discomfort of going through customs, long airport waits and turbulent skies was made a little easier. Frank had fixed Heap up somehow to get him across, but it was still a relief to have that behind them.

"If I think about this at all, I start wondering why I'm doing it," said Audrey.

"Because you want to see your sister. And give her the note."

"But you could have done that. This isn't like me at all. I haven't wanted to see her in twenty years." Audrey took out her boarding passes for the fourth time to make sure everything was in order. "I wonder if I'm changing."

"Maybe," said Heap. He munched on stale pistachios that had cost him five dollars. They were in Minneapolis now, where there was a three-hour layover. "Or maybe you're just being your real self."

Audrey looked at Heap and felt a surge of good will towards him.

"Maybe. Like what Lily's being."

"Yeah, maybe."

"The Lily you describe isn't the one I know."

"Maybe she just isn't the one you've seen lately," said Heap.

Audrey laughed. "You're waxing awfully philosophical this morning. You sound frightfully wise."

"Well, it's just that I've seen Honey change lately. For the better, I mean. And it couldn't have come from nowhere. I think she's changed into who she used to be. And the Lily you talk about doesn't sound much like the one I know, so I suspect something similar may have happened there."

"You're a smart guy, Heap."

He laughed. "That's the first time anyone's ever spoken those words in my direction."

"Smart and good too."

Someone had called him good before and Heap thought of her now with her hair cut short and her new dog. After Audrey was straightened away he would keep on going, down to Mexico where things would slow down again. Iris would be glad to see him, wanting to hear his news, and the sun would be so hot, the way it never got up here.

Heap ate pistachios and Audrey fig newtons to tide them over to the next in-flight snack.

"What if she's not glad to see me?" Audrey asked.

"She will be."

"What if she's not, though?"

"Then you turn around and go back home." Heap

sauntered over to the departure screen to see if their flight was on time. It was, so they joined the throngs on the moving walkway for the next leg of the journey.

It was dusk when they reached their destination, and the trip had exhausted them, so they decided to leave their mission till the next day.

Heap showed her the way. Every time she crossed the river she smelled the lakes of her youth. The warm wind in spring was like a long-ago, other-side thing. She found it hard to bear.

She walked down the crooked street with no curbs till she came to a house as bent and twisted as the road. All on one floor, it had been built onto haphazardly in more than one place by someone who didn't care about continuity or proportion. It needed paint and the fence did too, in the parts where it was wooden. There were sections of stone and a bit of chain-link to keep it from being too pretty.

Audrey wanted to live in this house, or one just like it. She pictured her straight, painted storey-and-a-half on her cold suburban street and wondered where she had been when her life had gone by.

She knocked on the door, taking off her sweater as she waited, wishing she had brought more summery clothes. Her jeans and runners were too much and she felt the heat. She wiped her forehead on her sleeve and imagined herself in a cotton dress with a tan and no shoes.

No one answered so she followed the dirt path to the backyard. What an odd neighbourhood this was. The house next door looked like Diana should have been waving from the window. And on her way down the street Audrey had spotted a limousine and chauffeur idling in a driveway. Yet there were other houses like this one too, like turnips among the corn.

Honey held the ladder while Lillian ran her hands along the eaves, hauling out decaying lumps of blackened vegetation and splatting them to the ground.

Audrey watched the tanned shape of her sister diligently performing this task. They wore overalls, the two of them, Lily's arms lean and brown, Honey's soft, rounded and pale. And they held the tools and squinted up at the sun; they were a couple. Audrey was jealous at first of the clear friendship and then she was just happy when she looked at the beautiful brown creature Lily had become.

Finally they spotted her and gave her lemonade and Peak Freans and a bed for the night. In the cool southern morning she lay on a lawn chair with her face turned toward the sky. The sun shone through the cypress, warming her off and on between the leaves. She slept briefly and woke to the sound of her sister calling her name. She knew it was a good thing, that this dear familiar voice had always been there and that she too had always been there, listening.